Janet Carlson Calvert Library
Franklin, CT 06254

DATE DUE

The Letters

The Letters

LUANNE RICE
JOSEPH MONNINGER

Bantam Books

THE LETTERS
A Bantam Book / October 2008

Published by Bantam Dell
A Division of Random House, Inc.
New York, New York

Book design by Virginia Norey

Bantam Books is a registered trademark of Random House, Inc.,
and the colophon is a trademark of Random House, Inc.

Library of Congress Cataloging-in-Publication Data
Rice, Luanne.
The Letters / Luanne Rice & Joseph Monninger.
p. cm.
ISBN 978-0-553-80741-7
1. Spouses—Fiction. 2. Bereavement—Fiction. 3. Adult children—
Death—Fiction. I. Monninger, Joseph. II. Title.

PS3568.I289L48 2008
813'.54—dc22
2008025627

Printed in the United States of America
Published simultaneously in Canada

www.bantamdell.com

BVG   10 9 8 7 6 5 4 3 2 1

The Letters

POLARIS

✳

If I could put my hand on the north star,
would it be as beautiful?

—Ralph Waldo Emerson

November 6

Dear Hadley,

I made it. I suppose it would be more accurate to say I can see how I *will* make it in the next few days. I am at the last stage, as far as the planes can take me, at a fishing camp called Laika Star. From here I travel by dogsled, a prospect that both thrills me and fills me with no small amount of fear. You remember how I loved Jack London and read it to Paul when he was ten? Suddenly the prospect of a real mush stands before me, and I am not as intrepid as I believed myself to be. Strange when dreams come face to face with reality. I am to meet the dog driver tomorrow. She will go over my equipment and supply anything else that I need. It should take about ten days, which is a long time to be in the Alaskan bush in winter.

I think of you often here. I'm not sure you would like this country. Alaska is vast and lonely and haunting. It's one thing to hear about it, another to travel it. Most of the state's population lives near Anchorage or Fairbanks. Good roads connect those two cities, but the rest of the state relies on planes. You know all that, of course. I'm sorry if I'm telling you more or less than you need to know. It's been years—back to our courtship, really—since I wrote you a true letter. And I am beyond email, or any electronic communication. Even to call would take a satellite phone, and I suspect we should stand by our decision to take a break for a while to sort out what our marriage means or how it should end. Letters seem like a more reasoned way to communicate. I hope you understand and I hope you'll write back.

I also wanted to say I know you think this trip is a bad idea. I understand. I do. But I have to see where he died, honey. I just do. I don't know if it will change anything, or bring me any peace, but I feel I must do it. I can't go forward until I know more. I want to know how he spent his last days, and what he thought and felt, as least as far as such things are knowable. I'm sorry if my need to do this causes you pain.

On a lighter note, I should mention that you would like my cabin. It is a model of efficiency and low-tech elegance. Everything is fashioned out of logs, like a boy's dream of a Lincoln Log cabin. Martha Stewart meets Sergeant Preston of the Yukon! A Vermont Castings stove sits in one corner, and you can open the doors to the stove and it becomes a fireplace. Beautiful, really. I have it running now and the room smells of cedar and pine and oak. The beds are firm and the linens top quality. The trout and salmon fishing around here is world-class, I gather, and they routinely fly in some big names. In the dining room I've seen pictures of

Bobby Knight, the famous basketball coach, and George Bush Sr. The proprietor, a man named Gus—shouldn't all proprietors be named Gus?—pointed out a dozen more photographs, but I just nodded and did my best to appear impressed, because clearly I was supposed to know who they were. TV stars, I guess. I didn't recognize any of them, and that simply confirms that I am hopelessly out of date.

I am eager to hear your news, but I will understand if you decide not to write back. I am not trying to gloss over the troubles we've had in our marriage. I understand that we may not be capable of mending our life together. I want you to know that I am sorry for my part in our rifts, and that as hurtful as I have been at times, it was never my intention to do anything but love you. I failed, of course, but I did not mean to fail.

More tomorrow.

Sam

Hadley—

I have a way to get the mail quickly to you, as remarkable as that must seem for someone writing from the Alaska outback. Gus puts his mail on the regular plane to Anchorage, but the bush plane operators provide a FedEx connection. FedEx does an overnight thing, and if it all hits correctly you can get mail to anyone in the lower forty-eight in about three days. They claim when it works right it is faster, if more expensive, than regular mail. So I want to get this in an envelope before I go to bed.

Before I tell you about meeting the dogs, and the wonder of all that, I have to tell you a funny anecdote. It turns out that you have to feed a woodstove all night! I must sound like a bumbling idiot, but I went to bed without giving it a thought, assuming, I suppose, that Gus had some form of backup heat. I woke at two in the morning and I have never been colder in my life! I don't know what I was thinking. Plain stupid, really. Stocked properly, the stove can easily make it through the night and keep the cabin warm, but I didn't think twice before going to sleep. So, you would have watched your husband on his hands and knees, blowing carefully onto a twist of paper and tinder, trying to get the last dying embers to flame up. I did it, too, and I have never seen a more welcome sight than those first few flames. I fed that fire with more tenderness, more attention, than I have lavished on anything in years. (That sounds horrible...I should lavish attention and tenderness on you, shouldn't I?) But you know what I mean. Eventually the fire got going and I filled the stove full, and the cabin is so well insulated it began warming up in no time. I glanced out the window at a thermometer on the porch post and saw it had dropped to −10. Cold, but not as cold as it will get. Not by a long shot. I climbed back under the blankets, and sat up in bed and gauged the heat as it moved slowly through the cabin. Wonderful, wonderful heat. I tried to go back to sleep, but I felt restless, and a little excited to be meeting the dogs in the morning, so I read a while, *The Three Musketeers*, of all things, but I couldn't quite get involved. I finally gave it up and I slid out of bed one more time to open the doors on the stove. You can imagine the wonderful light the fire gave. I hustled back into bed and watched the flames for a long time and I felt a million things.

I felt young, sweetheart. That might sound crazy to you, but I did. Propped up on the pillows, watching the flames, about a dozen Hudson Bay blankets weighing me down, I thought about you, us, our student days in Providence. Do you remember that art project the RISD student did on Benefit Street? He talked the town administrators into letting him cover a block of that beautiful old street with grass sod and then brought in two enormous Jersey cows, their udders virtually dragging on the ground, and for one afternoon and evening the street became a rural countryside again. I thought it was brilliant in its way; it made us look at the street with a different perspective. Anyway, I've never told you, but I think that's the first time I saw you. I know we met later, and we talk about that as our first meeting and I never wanted to spoil that, but I have a memory of you, or a dream, and you are dressed in black—a black skirt and a turtleneck—and you are riding one of the first English bikes I ever saw, with handlebar brakes, and you ride by on the other side of the street. It doesn't really matter if it's true or not, but I swear you entered my consciousness that day. You were so beautiful. Your hair was in a French braid and you looked straight ahead, not particularly solid on the bike, and I saw you as if somehow magically you had brought the countryside to good old Providence, and it was something out of Thomas Hardy, a girl with radiant skin, and serious knees, pumping away down the street. I never told you before because I've never known if I imagined it, or had dreamed it into being, and besides, I remember our real first meeting vividly, too. In any case, you were tremendously present in the cabin with me, alone in Alaska, both of us far down under the covers.

Sam

Hadley—

You must think I've completely lost my mind.

After my strange night—you really were in the cabin, you know, but a younger you, a college girl you—I woke early. I should tell you a little about Gus. He lives out here by himself. He has a girlfriend, but she refuses to spend the winter so far north. She retreats to Anchorage and visits him now and then, but only when the weather permits. She is a pilot, so she can buzz up here when she likes. Her name is Cindy. She spends the summers here, working as a pilot and a guide. He does all the cooking, the grounds work, and so on. They hire a crew of kids to serve as kitchen help, and they pay them top dollar. It's prestigious, I gather, to work at Laika Star. The kids pass down the jobs to brothers and sisters. The season is short, but they make a killing because of the fishing. The river near here, the Yankawalett (an Inuit name), has the finest grayling fishing in North America. People try to collect different fish the way old-time hunters collected big-game heads, and grayling, with an outsized dorsal fin, are a must. Fly-fishing, according to Gus, has become wildly popular, and plenty of CEOs and corporate bigwigs don't think twice about dropping a pile of dough to get to remote rivers. That's how Gus gets by.

(Don't worry, by the way...I have winter rates, which are much more reasonable.)

Gus fixed breakfast in the main lodge. When I asked if it wasn't a bit extravagant to keep the lodge heated during the winter, he mentioned that he expected a snowmobile party in ten days' time, and if he let the heat go out the cold would sink into the wood and it would be the devil to get heated again. Cheaper, he said, to keep it going. So we had the enormous lodge to ourselves, and Gus ate with me—ham, bacon, eggs, beans, sourdough toast, and oatmeal. I didn't feel hungry when I sat down at the table, but I ate and ate and ate, and I still don't know why. Maybe the good air.

Gus resembles every minor prospector character in every western you've ever seen. You know the type: gray beard, sharp, birdy features, a wide, wrinkled forehead, and a pair of red suspenders. Small and wiry. His right index finger is missing at the second joint, and his right foot lags out a little as if he wanted to ease a small dog forward with it. He's aware that he plays to type, but he's also perilously close to being a type, so it all works together in a funny sort of way. When he brought in breakfast I expected him to start babbling about gold in them thar hills, but he satisfied himself with sliding the food onto the table and that was that.

Good food, too. Nothing fancy, but he took pride in what he served. He told me he has an order in for a haunch of moose meat for the snowmobile party. They asked for it. He'll make some stews and a chili with it. Moose meat makes more sense up here than standard beef, he said, especially in winter.

The next part is about Paul. So skip it if it's too painful to read. But Gus knew a little about the accident from his girlfriend, Cindy, who knows all the pilots. It's a small world up here, not in land, but in population, so it wasn't surprising that he knew a few things. He fished around a little to figure out what I was doing up here by myself in the winter, trying to figure how I would take it, I guess, but then he told me what he knew. So here goes.

He never met Paul. Paul waited in Anchorage for three days, hoping to get decent weather. The school year up on the northern slope had a start date of September 1. I guess it's customary to buy all your groceries before going that far north, and people don't think twice about hiring planes. Paul was heading into the arctic night, which can be paralyzing, according to Gus. And the village where Paul was going to teach—I can't come close to spelling the name, but it's something like Ukallatahal—had the usual problems with alcoholism and domestic abuse and a dozen other things. They also fared miserably with the Alaskan oil rights. That is a very long story—and Gus told me most of it—but it's enough to say the village had money from oil rights, lost it, appealed to the government for protection, lost money again, and wound up back where it had begun.

Paul had new textbooks for his classes, and a year's worth of school materials. I like knowing that small detail and I hope you do, too.

Gus said the consensus held that ice had brought the

plane down. That concurs with the official report. He said that dozens of planes go down every year, most from ice or some outside factor. He even said geese bring some planes down by flocks flying into them, and so on. They fly Otters up here, like the one Paul was in, and Otters are exceptionally reliable planes. But conditions are difficult and if you get in trouble, as Paul's plane did, you have nowhere to emergency land unless you can get to a lake. The pilot, from what Gus knew from Cindy, was experienced and steady. Irish Canadian, as you know. (I've blocked his name right now . . .)

That's all so far. I understand you think this quest of mine is self-punishing, or masochistic, but I feel I have to go through with it. I pushed him to do something different, to try something adventurous. And our beautiful son ended up dead.

I have to stop now.

Sam

November 10

Dear Sam,

I got your letter. I'm glad you made it there safely.
Thanks, I guess, for letting me know.

Hadley

Still Nov. 10 . . .

Dear Sam,

Well, that was rotten of me. I'm sorry, I really am. I ran to catch the mail boat (yes, you read that right), but I was too late. It was just chugging away from the dock, disappearing into the fog. Honestly, it couldn't have been more symbolic—me standing on the wharf, waving and yelling, while my letter to you disappears into the great unknown. Sound familiar? Sorry again. I'll try not to sound bitter.

Okay, take two. I got your letter. And you're right—it came fast, via FedEx. The thing was, it went home (it being home, you probably figured that's where I'd be). But I'm not. I'm in a tiny, drafty, salt-soaked cottage on Monhegan Island. Jenny saw the truck arrive from next door and intercepted the envelope. She had them forward it here, to Monhegan. Expensive way to get mail. I can almost hear your rationale—you're in

13

Alaska, but it's my trip, too, and you want to keep me up on the details as you learn them.

It's beautiful on the island. I came out at the beginning of October, have been here almost a month and a half now—I just knew I needed to get away. I tell myself it's not because of you, or because you've undertaken such a journey—such a pilgrimage. I honestly believe, with all the soul-searching I can muster (and you know I can muster plenty—no comments, please), that my coming here was all on my own, nothing at all to do with you.

Are you ready? I'm painting again.

That's why I chose Monhegan—in the summer, there's a real, true, working artists' colony here. By the time I got here, the artists were starting to leave, head home. That's okay— the desolation suits me right now. Jamie Wyeth has a house at one end of the island, and there are constant Jamie sightings, although I myself haven't seen him. It's a little how I imagine things might have been in Honfleur back in the days of Monet... "Did you see Claude?" "Claude just picked up his mail." "Claude is down by the haystacks." Etc. Jamie has that kind of allure and fame. I don't care about Jamie's allure and fame. I just care that I've picked up a paintbrush again.

The cottage is a shambles, but I love it. I rented it from an ad in the *Boston Globe*—two lines mentioning a sunflower garden and a water view. Even when I first got here, the sunflowers were dead. The water view requires jimmying a lock, climbing the ricketiest attic stairs you've ever seen, and leaning out the window to spy a distant patch of harbor between bare branches and pine boughs. When I called the owner to ask what the hell, he apologized and told me he hadn't been there in a while, then offered to sell me the cottage for what sounds to me like a song. Seems he inherited it from his recently deceased mother—who was an artist and knew, of course, Jamie.

I told him I'd think it over. The truth, Sam, is that I want it. I can see myself here, and I haven't been able to see myself anywhere. The kitchen smells of linseed oil and turpentine; the walls are lined with my landlord's mother's paintings. She was something of a primitive, but with poetry and soul—think Grandma Moses meets Gauguin. With a touch of Georgia O'Keeffe. Sutton, her son and my landlord, said she was a "character," and something in his tone makes me know there's much more to it.

I feel her presence with me. Almost as if she's protecting, guiding me into these long, cold months. There's something about the way the November weather on this island far at sea matches what I've been feeling inside since Paul died. I think she would understand. She signed her paintings "A." That's all—just A. So I feel I have the ghost of A here with me.

She's with me right now, as I write this letter to you. I think I need her, too. This isn't easy. Reading your letter from Laika Star, my hands are shaking. You're really there? *Why?*

You say you hope I understand, but I don't. You want me to know you know I think it's a bad idea, and I do. What good can come from it? As much time as I've had to think about it, as hard as you've tried to persuade me, I still come back to the same thing: Alaska killed him.

You asked me to write back (aren't you sorry?), so that's what I'm doing. He was so dear and tender. He loved the outdoors, but never as much as you wanted him to. He wanted to save the world, but why couldn't he have waited to graduate and then done that here in Maine, or New Hampshire, or Arkansas, or Texas, or any of the places Teach for America would have sent him? Why did he have to choose the most remote place on the globe?

Please don't let's keep this up. I can't bear going back and forth with you on this; I hear myself seeming to blame you and realize that's *just* what I'm doing. We loved him more than air. And we buried him. He's gone, Sam—and you being there does nothing to change that.

Have a drink with Gus, and turn for home. I've decided I don't want the house. You can have it—I'll tell Charlie, and he can work it all out with your lawyer. I really do like it here. The winter might be tough, but I don't care. The first snow fell last week, and I climbed up to the attic and stared at it falling on the harbor.

Hadley

P.S. If you're going to write again, send letters to me at
3 Lupine Hill Road
Monhegan Island, Maine 04852

You know I don't agree with you on any of it—it's your quest, not mine, I never wanted you to go. So I give you permission to ask why I'm replying in the same way, overnight express. The truth is, I don't know. Perhaps I just want to do my part in playing out this last act of ours.

*

Be careful. I didn't say that before.

But please, can you be careful up there? We may be apart now, but that doesn't mean I want both of you dying in that wilderness.

I have to run to catch the boat, to get this off to you.

Hadley

Dear Sam,

I can't decide whether fate has taken a hand in the timing of our correspondence. You're writing me at home, and in spite of the strange magic of getting the mail back and forth from Alaska at warp speed, it's still delayed, so your letters continue as if you haven't received my replies. It's almost funny because you're being so nice and I'm being so not. What is that song from the Sondheim musical—"Send in the Clowns"? It's about bad timing, missed opportunities—Judy Collins sang it. You made fun of me for liking it. But then again, you always did think I was too sentimental, that I saw life as a Hallmark card waiting to happen. Not anymore though, right? Not after what happened to Paul.

So. You and the woodstove. You kept her going all night. I have to admit you were right—my hackles went up (the only time I ever even think of hackles is with you, which has to say something . . .) when you wrote about lavishing all that tenderness on that stove. Maybe it's even seeing the word "tenderness" on a page written by you.

I'm used to seeing your dispatches from the ring—or the field, or the mountain, or the surf break—whatever story you're covering, whatever extreme athlete you're writing about. I think of your work as muscular and rigorous, hard-hitting and incisive. That piece you did on Brooks Robinson?

You could have been writing about yourself. So...tenderness...I'm so not used to seeing it flow from your pen.

The way you described the fire.

You know, it's a cold night here. Lots of fog. When a fog bank rolls in off the Atlantic, it slams into the high seaward-facing cliffs, then covers the island. You've never seen fog this thick; when I walk outside and look down, I can't see my feet. I want to paint on the rocks, to take my easel out to the bluffs, but it's been too wet. I feel soaked through. So reading your letter...Sam, I lit a fire in the fireplace.

It's burning now.

I guess it makes me feel connected with you. I don't know why I'm writing that. I'm sure I'll mail this letter and then want to take it back. But what you wrote...about tending the stove, and the heat you felt, and the Hudson Bay blankets...it made me long for warmth. I've been so cold.

Are the blankets those beautiful white ones, with the colored stripes on top? Narrow bands of color—red, blue, green, yellow. Those blankets? Remember when we went to Nantucket that time, way before Paul was born, so you could fish for stripers? And I grabbed a blanket to wrap around us at the beach? It was one of those...Hudson Bay, I'm sure of it.

That memory of me. Why did you decide to tell me about it now? We're half a world apart, and Charlie's calling what's your lawyer's name to tell him I'm giving you the house, and I'm finally painting again. I had to leave you for that to happen, Sam. I had to stop thinking of Paul. So here I am with the ghost of an old lady painter, feeling almost happy for the first time in I don't know how long, and you say "tenderness" and you write me a memory of me.

Maybe it's the fire, and maybe it's the tea—yes, I'm drinking tea. Still. Seventy-nine days. But I remember the first time I saw you, too. You were sitting at a table at Penguins, that funny little café on Thayer Street. There were some girls from the Brown writing program at the booth behind you, talking about Robert Coover in that worshipful way students always talked about him.

You seemed oblivious. You were just sitting there, writing in a black notebook. Your head was down, and you were concentrating. You wore a thick green sweater, and jeans. You wore boots. I took all that in, because you looked out of place. Even before you glanced up, I knew you'd have a beard—and you did. You had sharp, piercing eyes that looked at me as if—I swear, this is how it felt—I were a refugee from a war-torn land, and it was your job to tell my story.

Actually, I was about to write "it was your job to save me," but I think, to you, they're the same thing. You looked older than the other students, as if you'd seen too much already. Little did I know you were a sportswriter; in spite of that, you were—and are—an old soul.

I stared at you, because I wanted to draw you. Well, I wanted to know you—then draw you. I thought if I could capture the intensity of your stare, if I could get that down in charcoal, it would nail my life-drawing grade. Forget the nude, forget the draped chair—those eyes, your eyes were the essence of life.

I should have known then, Sam—I couldn't capture anything about you. Not in charcoal, not in oils, not with my heart, not with my love. So you and your tenderness—I don't want to hear it. You're in the wild, where you're happiest. On the edge of the world and the extremity of life. Maybe you write about sports, outdoor activities, but you go after the internal landscape of your subjects—as well as your own—with something of the war correspondent. Everyone's always risking everything. Surfers surfing eighty-foot waves at Ghost Tree, climbers clinging to the Eiger with nothing but air between them and oblivion. And considering the collateral damage of Paul's plane, you've made your way to another war zone.

Let me tell you something . . . and I really do say this as someone who knows you. I know you're there to save someone. It's what you try to do in your writing, it's what you think *Harper's* pays you for, what you think those awards are about. You're up in Laika Star with Gus and the stove and *The Three Musketeers*, and you're feeding the fire, and you're dreaming of something so long past . . . and you're there to save someone.

You know he's gone.

All you have to do is reread your letter to know. Ice

brought the plane down. That's what you said; it's there on the page, in your handwriting. Do I have to remind you he wasn't one of your professional adventurers? He was up there to teach. To help others. He wasn't trying to break any records, be the daringest. Our boy wasn't trying to tempt fate—he was just trying to help others with so much less than he had escape theirs...fates of poverty and hopelessness. He was there to help people get *out* of that wilderness. Don't you know that?

Sam, let him go.

And let me go, too.

We have to live again, and it's not happening. Not yet. We're both frozen. Paul's plane went down, and we're in the glacier. So if there's any saving to do, save yourself.

Stop this.

Hadley

Hadley—

Dogs, dogs, dogs! (Sorry to have been so gloomy in my last.)

I'll write this up quickly, then throw it in the mail. Gus informed me that the special mail carrier, a bush pilot named Dixie, will swing by soon. She won't wait for anything, so we must have our letters ready.

I don't know where to begin. Gus took me over on a snowmobile to Martha Rich's "Dog Driving School and Adventure-Staging Platform." What a name! And what a woman! She is tiny, to begin with. When you meet her you think, well, this can't be right. But when you check her resume, you realize she has been to the north and south poles, both by dog team, and she was profiled by the BBC when she led an all-woman team up Mount McKinley. She is forty-five, maybe, and has reddish features and hair, a kind of Irish colleen only shrunk down and made more pocket-sized, and more dense and firm, and determined. She had a tight handshake, a steady eye, and she took me immediately to see the dogs.

And when you see her with the dogs, then you understand.

I read a long time ago that when Mother Teresa passed among the poor, she touched them. Every one of them. Her hands never stopped. I know it's a strange connection to make, but that's what came to mind when I saw Martha Rich among her dogs. Beautiful dogs. She runs only Eskimo dogs,

23

an indigenous breed that goes back, literally, to the Stone Age. They are short, stocky animals, but possess blazing eyes. She introduced me to them all, or at least as many as I could see, and each one had a personality and a presence.

She told me a thousand things and I can't repeat them all here, or remember them, but the long and short of it is that it shouldn't be a hard passage. Five days in, five days out, she figures. Honestly, I think she sees it as a training run for some of the dogs. She will bring two sleds, ten dogs each, and all the equipment. (She doesn't trust anyone else's equipment, by the way, so she discarded 97 percent of everything I brought. This is not her first rodeo, as the saying goes, so I simply nodded and took her advice.) She wasn't short or nasty about anything, but neither did she tiptoe around or mince words. I liked her. She knew exactly what she was about.

When we arrived back at Laika Star, Gus told me that Martha sews her own tents, blends her own dog food, designs her own stoves, and a dozen other tricks of the trade. She is probably one of the top ten polar explorers alive today. I knew some of this, but I didn't know it all, and now I feel privileged to be traveling with her.

Okay, I have to hurry and get this in the mail. Whether we go forward together or not, I love you. Write to me if you can. I will tell you more about the dogs soon.

Sam

November 13

Sam—

Martha Rich? Hand-sewn tents?
What are you doing?

Hadley

P.S.
Look. Be careful. You're crazed, do you realize that?
Comparing Martha Rich, whoever she is, to Mother
Teresa—Martha Rich's hands touching the dogs, never stop-
ping, the way Mother Teresa's hands touched the poor,
never stopping. Jesus, Sam!!

You know, my faith died the day Paul did. I didn't want to
hear about the saints or the faithful, or people who believe
in God and His mercy, His infinite mercy. But you know
what I just read? Just a few weeks ago, in someplace ridiculous, like *People* magazine or somewhere, that Mother Teresa
was a fraud. Okay, maybe that's too strong. But they found
some letters of hers, or a diary, and it turns out she stopped
believing in God decades ago—she was tormented with love
for someone she no longer believed existed. She had a crisis
of faith, stopped believing for a time, continued to question
her belief and life's choices. And you know what? That made
me like her.

She faked the last fifty years of her life. Wearing that habit, receiving the archbishops and cardinals and the Pope himself, and all those people who set her up on a pedestal, seeming to pray and believe in the Lord, and in Jesus the Savior, and in all the angels and archangels. Boy, did she pull a fast one! All that time, pretending to go along with the dogma, she was wracked by doubt. There must have been anguish, hidden behind her veil.

Dark night of the soul, baby. Me and Mother Teresa. And Jesus, for that matter. "Help thou mine unbelief." The only line in the Bible I can stand.

So whatever this Martha Rich person has to offer, I hope she gets you where you want to go. Two sleds, twenty dogs, you and she on the tundra. What a story that will make . . . I have this strange, clear image of you *going*. As in going someplace, yes, but also leaving. You're leaving by dogsled.

And what are you leaving, Sam? I guess I could ask myself the same question: what are we leaving behind and why? A lot of love, that's for sure. There was so much love. There had to be, to explain the crash—not the moment Paul's plane fell from the sky, but the aftermath. What happened to us afterward. What we did to each other . . . and to ourselves.

We were so solid for so long—or were we? Now I'm questioning all we had, everything we seemed to be. Weren't we the perfect couple, the ones everyone looked at to figure out how we did it? Our house, the orchard . . . those were the outward trappings. But the inside stuff was pretty great, too. The way we talked and laughed, the way I'd pull you away from your desk and make you take me for a ride. I'd love those times in the truck, when no one could get to us. Not even Paul . . . It was just us.

But who were we? That's what is tormenting me now. If we were so great, why did we fall apart just when—you'd think—we needed each other most? I was an idiot, and I admit it. But you were so rotten to me. I never felt you'd ever forgive me ever. Ever. I keep picturing a beautiful sweater, like the ones I knit for you and Paul when I was on that Icelandic kick. Remember? That gorgeous ice-colored wool, shades of white and gray, spun from the fleece of arctic yaks or some such creature. I'd be knitting a sleeve and find a bramble caught in the yarn and know it came from a sheep tramping through the great north beyond.

Those sweaters always seemed so sturdy, so durable. Nothing could ever happen to them. But all it takes is a pull—one little snag on a nail or a branch—and one stitch comes undone. Then another, then more, and suddenly you have a ladder of destruction, the whole thing falling apart. A sweater, sure—but *us*? That's what I feel happened to you and me, to us. Hadley and Sam, good old solid us. One pull, one stitch—a big one for sure, but still. We could have picked up the stitch, couldn't we have?

Why am I talking about sweaters? It's all so sad and

stupid. We're done, we're over, those old sweaters are in mothballs if they still exist at all. Who knows what you did with yours, and I can't remember seeing Paul's after he left for Amherst. Lumps of wool, a big pile of dust. All of it.

November 13 late

(I feel I've been writing you all day . . .)

Dear Sam,

Okay, that was the longest P.S. in the history of the writ-ten word.

Cooler heads always seem to prevail, but only after the mail boat has left. I feel like a twenty-year-old, writing let-ters, having second thoughts, running to get them back—only to discover it's too late.

I'm sorry, Sam. My words have been harsh, and I don't mean them to sound that way—well, mostly I don't.

I'm in such a beautiful and fragile place. The island, I mean . . . but maybe also my spirit. You know I broke in half after Paul . . . he fell from the sky, and so did I. Knowing that you were going to the place where he died—Sam, I can't tell you what that made me feel. A combination of terror, shame, and gratitude.

Terror that the same thing might happen to you, shame because I'm not there with you, I can't find the strength to lay eyes on the spot where it happened, and gratitude—I tell you this reluctantly, because I don't want it to spur you on, don't want to make you go somewhere you otherwise wouldn't. The more I think about it, or rather, dream about it, the more I'm glad that you're there to be with him. With Paul.

Because I know where we buried his body, Sam, but that place you're heading is where his spirit lives . . . In the place he died. I believe that. It gives me peace of sorts. His body . . . that wasn't him. We couldn't see anything of our boy in what came back to us. Sometimes I wish I hadn't even looked. The memory of what I saw at the funeral home that day drained my heart. The most hope I've had in so long has just started to come from thinking of you going to meet him—to connect with his beautiful spirit. There was light snow last night, and it dusted the pine boughs . . . Here's a drawing of what I can see out my window right now, to thank you for going to Paul.

I found out the name of my ghost. She's Annabelle Frost. Sutton told me that she was eighty-three, a member of the Boston Art Club and American Watercolor Society, and the Society of American Artists. She was the real deal. She divorced Sutton's father, fell in love with a man who lived here on Monhegan, moved to the island to be near him. She died right in this house, last December.

Sutton was afraid to tell me—that I'd be spooked and want to leave. But I feel the opposite. It comforts me, makes me realize she's nearby. I know her spirit is right here, Sam— just as I know Paul's spirit is near Ukallatahal. So it soothes me, in a way I'm just beginning to let myself feel, to know that you will be near him.

Annabelle helps me realize this . . .

Don't think I'm going round the bend. I swear I haven't been this sane in years. Eighty days without a drink, for one thing. There's a little church here on the island, and I've been going to AA. I know you think I'm not an alcoholic—in fact, I noticed how you wrote about the alcoholism of the Eskimos, wondered how you'd feel knowing your wife was one, too—but I am. I'm not sure when I crossed the invisible line; I imagine it was sometime during that year after . . . There was before, and there was after. I started drinking to black out after. But you know all that . . .

I like the group here. It's small and vigorous. One old lobsterman's been sober for thirty-nine years. And he said he was still drinking at his fortieth birthday . . . I do the math and feel daunted. I try to stick with "one day at a time."

The slogans are so hokey; it embarrasses me to repeat them. Again, back to me the sentimentalist. You must think it's ridiculous, that I can buy into a group that would measure out wisdom—not with Eliot's coffee spoons—but in pithy sayings tacked up to church basement walls. I can just feel you cringing . . .

But it seems to be working for me. They tell you to remember the day you hit bottom. I don't have to think very far. The accident, of course. But so many other things. The way I started to disappear. The way you'd turn to me—I'd see those piercing eyes I used to long to draw—and just want to close mine, so I couldn't see you. My own version of the hole in the sweater, the stitches starting to pull. You remind me so of Paul . . . He had his own intensity, not for the written word, but for teaching/helping/saving . . . in those ways he was his father's son.

Hitting bottom . . .

I remember, Sam. Sometimes I think I haven't quite hit it yet—the true bottom might come along with the divorce papers. Do you ever think that? What it will be like to pick up a pen and end our life together? Oh, that might just be me being sentimental again—I guess I ended it the day of the accident. Or maybe you did, the day you moved out. I've lost track.

In any case, I have something to tell you. I'm buying the cottage. The price is crazy-low. I can paint here. I *want* you to have the house—or maybe you can't bear to keep it either. Maybe we were too happy there for either of us to stay.

The island is beautiful. Back in October, when I first got here, the sun was out almost continuously. I spent the first two weeks painting *en plein air*. I'd set up my easel in the meadow, a field of flowers right in the center of town. Later I went to White Head, one of the high cliffs across the island. The other painters would gather, and it was quite a scene.

As I told you, most everyone leaves for the winter, but a few have stayed. One artist, John Morgan, I remember from RISD. We bump into each other at the grocery store, but he keeps to himself. People who stay the winter here aren't looking for company.

The island is even more amazing now. It's lonely and windswept and haunting. It's inspiring. Even the names of the places—Cathedral Woods, Swim Beach, the Ice Pond, the Tercentenary Tablet. There are seals, which means you-know-what. There's a lighthouse and a shipwreck. It's a brutal, rocky coast: gray boulders, white foam, the endless sea, and whatever is swimming beneath . . .

Oh—and there's a cat. A hungry, stray cat that sits on the stone wall behind my cottage. She stares as if she wants something from me. But when I approach, she runs away. What should I do? You were always magic when it came to animals . . . She's a little gray tiger.

Be safe, Sam. When you get to the place, will you tell him I love him?

Watch out for icefalls and Martha Rich.

Hadley

November 18

Hadley—

Your letters arrived today in one big bundle. I admit I am annoyed and more than a little hurt, but glad to receive them nonetheless. I am feeling a dozen other emotions I can't begin to sort out. Confused, mostly. How can you still cause this turmoil in me?

I need to think about what I want to say. And I'll confess right now that I wasn't entirely honest before. I am not sorry if this trip upsets you; or at least I can't entertain that thought right now. I need to be here. I need to visit Paul. Call it his spirit, his ghost, whatever it might be. If he somehow exists in heaven or Valhalla or wherever he is, I want him to know that I came looking for him. That I stood next to his last earthly place and greeted his spirit. That his father came to find him.

Stopping now . . .

*

Deep breath.

I've decided not to edit this, or to rethink it, or to delete things if they make me uncomfortable. We're past the need for editing, thank goodness. Say what you like. I'll say my piece. If I step over a line, or say something hurtful, I'm sorry. No pulled punches.

And while I'm thinking of it, and because you mentioned it, no, I don't think you are an alcoholic. What I think is, you are a lousy drunk when you get drunk. How's that? I hated to see your second drink go down, because the Hadley I loved, the wonderful woman I married, faded backward through your skin and ended up caged in your ribs. Nasty image. But that's what I felt. And then this other woman emerged, one I didn't like nearly as much, and she took over. I remember that time we went to Tankers, that restaurant on the old tanker ship outside of Portland. You had two martinis and the bartender looked at me when you ordered a third, and you snapped at him not to consult your husband, damn it, and then you held forth on tax codes, of all things, and by the end of it the couple we were with—the Babcocks, I think, the lovely, dashing Babcocks, what a pair—had grown glassy-eyed and uncomfortable and you didn't even see it. So that's my opinion on your drinking once and for all. It turned you into a bore. Not a drunk, just a bore.

*

I was tempted to cut that last part about your drinking, but then I said, no. Let it stand. I'm sure you have things to say to me. Fair enough. But I also need to be clear: I hated the drinking because it erased the woman I loved. The martini-you would never care about stopping on the road and cutting wildflowers, or putting a bouquet of black-eyed Susans on a picnic table when we camped—you did that in Idaho, remember, near the Henry's Fork. Do you know, if I could freeze one day, just one, from all our time together (not counting days with Paul), I would freeze the day beside the Henry's Fork. You spent the day in jeans and a red flannel shirt, with some sort of bandana in your hair, and you didn't care much about fishing, I know, but you loved the countryside, and you sketched an exquisite landscape all focused on a fence post and mountain perspective, and your cheeks were red and glowing, and that night we cooked rice and beans. And I had gone down to the river to fish and when I came back you were there at the campsite, and the sun was behind you, and you didn't see me for a second and I watched how beautifully you moved, how you had such purpose and calm, and you had cut an enormous bouquet of black-eyed Susans and arranged them in an old coffee tin sitting on the table. You had collected the flowers for no other reason except that you appreciated beauty, just beauty, and returning to you that way, coming toward the camp, I felt out of breath at the sight of you. If you remember, I kissed you and then I pushed you down on the table and I kissed you some more, and we stayed like that a long time, the mountains around us, and the first chill of evening coming on, and you didn't ask why, or what we were doing, and it didn't push on to sex. We just kissed, and I thought, still think, that you knew we were happy, and I did, and that we had the real thing, that we could arrange days just as you had arranged those flowers.

So, there. That's the other side. That's the you I lost when you had too much to drink.

Okay, turn the page. Next subject.

*

Are you still reading? Maybe I don't have the right to say such things to you. Tell me if I don't. Maybe I have surrendered that right.

Anyway, some news. I haven't left yet because the weather turned dirty and Martha—no worries there, I promise—came over to say we should postpone. She said we could slog it out, but we needed to wait until it "crisped up." By that, I suspect, she meant it had to freeze hard everywhere. The big danger in dogsledding, especially if you are bushwhacking, is unfrozen water. If you go through the ice, you're toast.

She came over and had dinner with me and Gus. A fun evening. Gus is an old crank, but he has a soft spot for Martha and he likes dogs. She brought over two house dogs—George and Sneak. Sneak is a sweet little female who, Martha claims, is the smartest dog she ever owned. And George is Sneak's boyfriend, I guess, and is a magnificent animal with a thick coat and eyes that you can hardly bear to look into.

The dogs walked all over the lodge, checking things, and you could tell they were dying to raise a leg and mark their territory, but they were just polite enough not to do it. Gus gave them each a bowl of moose meat and they ate it in greedy gulps. We took them out afterward, and we stood for a while watching the northern lights. Spectacular, really. Green slices of curtains. When we retreated back inside, the dogs went to sleep under the table like regular suburban dogs.

Martha gave us a little lecture on Global Positioning Systems, and we punched in the coordinates of Paul's accident. We have it fixed so I will know, as much as a person can know, when I am standing on the scene of his death. You can call me crazy, but it was important to me that I not pretend or guess about knowing the location. Now with a glance at Martha's GPS, we'll know for certain.

She also made a couple phone calls to people she trusted and got a long-range forecast, and she said we will likely get started soon. A fresh front is moving in and she liked the looks of it. It will be cold, she said, but dry and clear. All good.

So there. That's my news, such as it is.

I'm going to bed shortly. I'm writing this on an old typewriter. It's been years since I used a typewriter, but Gus had one around and he offered it to me. A manual Smith and

Corona. I'd forgotten how much I love that clickety-clack of typewriters. I feel a little like Jack Torrance in *The Shining*, typing away in a large, haunted lodge. If a little kid passes by on a Big Wheel, I'm out of here.

Sam

Hadley—

I want to say this: I could not be more pleased to hear you are painting again. I mean that. I have always loved your work, as you know, and to hear that you are painting again is like hearing an old friend has returned from being lost. Maybe that's a clumsy metaphor, but you know what I mean. You are a painter; painting is part of you. Even when you didn't paint, I knew you were storing it up, watching, taking mental notes. So I am not surprised, only delighted. One of the great pleasures in my life has been to sit near you, reading or writing, and to smell your paints and to look over and see you entirely absorbed. And then to look at the canvas— how astonishing it always was to see what you had created out of nothing, or from a suggestion of light and angles. I was always proud of your talent. I hope you know that. I hope I said it enough.

And now I have a wonderful image of you trekking out to the bluffs and plunking your easel down among the other painters, and maybe they aren't sure who this chick is, but she's good-looking, and then, little by little, they realize you are a master, and they start looking at their punky canvases and realize they should give it up...

That's my fantasy. But no matter what, the action of painting, the discipline of it, will be a joy to you. I know what you are like when you are painting. You begin to see everything with a greater clarity, and your movements become smooth and calm, and you are absolutely beautiful when you step back.

It might surprise you to know I am glad you are done with our house, and I am jealous of your new house on the island. I had a moment's sorrow when you talked about abandoning the house to me, because it was our house, Paul's house, but after a night's sleep I see the wisdom of it. It's time to move on. I am going to sell it and we can split the profits and go from there. It should bring a good price and it's never bad to have a pocketful of money. To my amazement, I don't feel much emotional attachment to the house. Isn't that odd? If anything, I feel attached to the trees we planted. Strange, I know. But I planted some of those trees with Paul, when he was little, and I will miss watching them go through the seasons. I suppose I can always visit and peek around like some sort of nosy neighbor. But you are right—as you are about many things—that we need to move forward.

I said that I am jealous of your house on Monhegan Island and I meant it. You belong next to the sea, and I can picture you with your ghost and your cat and the drafty parlor. I haven't even seen it, but I bet I can picture the light. One of the most endearing things about you—and you may not even be conscious of this—is that you are attracted to light the way plants follow sunlight. You are. I always thought part of your DNA was chlorophyll.

Have to stop here for a second. Gus came out to call me in to lunch.

*

It's set, I guess. I will leave Thursday with Martha Rich. Gus told me she radioed this morning. He is going to ride me over at sunrise that day. Then we leave right from her house. It's a bit unnerving to consider stepping out her back door and taking off, but there it is. I will be driving the second sled, following her lead. She assures me it is not as difficult to do as you might think, but the terrain we will eventually cross would clog and wreck a snowmobile. Dogsleds are more flexible if we need to bushwhack over some portions of the trail—and of course, it's a dream of mine to ride a dogsled in the North. I get the sense she doesn't anticipate any large delays. It's a workout for her dogs and not much more.

It's more complicated for me, but you know that.

Okay, I read your letters again and I think I am jealous of this John Morgan, your old friend from RISD. Actually, I've decided I have to punch him in the nose the minute I spot him. I'm joking, but I am jealous. Should I be? I have no right to ask that question—and you have no right to tell me to be wary of Martha Rich—but I can't seem to shake my green-eyed monster.

Enough of that.

I want you to know that I brought a photo of us—our family—with me. I will leave it there. You know the one: you, me, Paul, our cat, Boing, sitting on the tailgate of our old Ford pickup. Paul is holding Boing and he looks incredibly handsome—just the faint outline of the man he will become. And you have your arm around him, and I am back behind you both, reaching for something out of the camera range. I know you remember it. It was a great day.

I will leave the photo there, where Paul died. I hope you don't think that is morbid, or worse, too patently sentimental, but I need to carry something there, something to leave, even if it is a futile gesture. So now you know everything. That's my great plan. I wish I could explain it all better. I wish it had a more logical basis. It's just my heart. I can't help it.

Okay, I need a good night's sleep. I miss you and love you. I don't know where we're heading—you and me—but I am grateful for these letters. Say hello to Annabelle. Picture me in a red Mountie uniform, heading off into the brush!

Mush.

Sam

P.S. Nearly forgot. Tell me about the seals and the sharks—any sightings? Any stories? You know we have to talk about sharks.

Dear Sam,

Boing. Of all our cats, he was always, only, Paul's. The way they adopted each other on sight—Paul going out into the field the day after that fox had attacked the barn kittens' mother, the whole litter running as fast as they could away from him, turning feral already, but that one little tiger just breaking from the pack and leaping straight into his arms— boing. Tiny springs on his back paws . . .

And the way Paul would feed him with that little bottle you got from the vet. Doc McIntosh told you the kitten was too young, hadn't gotten enough antibodies from his mother's milk, was infested with fleas, had everything going against him, would need round-the-clock feeding and care that would be too much for a teenage boy . . . but you said he didn't know Paul. And you were right.

The alarm clock going off all through the night, every three hours. And the sound of Paul's bare feet on the hall floor, and then the ring of the microwave as he heated up the formula . . . and then sometimes I'd go downstairs to check, and he would have fallen asleep with the kitten in his arms—the two of them, our two young ones.

You picked the right picture to leave up there. You ask if I remember the day; of course I do. We'd just come home from that fishing trip to the Wind River, and Paul was getting ready to go back to Amherst, and we were all having one last picnic before summer ended. That light, and the way the ground was still warm from the summer sun. It was September, and we went to the orchard, and Boing chased bees, and we knew, *we knew*, what we had.

Chlorophyll in my DNA...if it's there, it's a mutation that occurred after I married you. Remember the year you fell in love with fruit trees? It was right after I got pregnant. I looked out the window one Saturday morning, and you were pulling in with twenty saplings tilting all over the truck bed. You spread the plaid blanket on the hillside so I could watch you planting them. I still have the sketchbook filled with all the drawings I did of you.

We never talked about why you did that—or if we did, I don't remember. Drawing your body, the strain in your shoulders as you worked, and the exultation in your whole being as you plunked the root balls down there in those deep holes you'd just broken your back to dig—I just, well, I just couldn't help feeling that it was all one and the same. I had Paul growing in me, and you needed something to nurture, too.

So the picture you brought to Alaska, that's the right one. Our picnic in the orchard, twenty years after you planted it...those first trees were all grown by then, and so was our boy. Almost grown, anyway.

The night after I read your most recent letter, I dreamed

about our orchard. It was fall, always our favorite time. The smell of apples was sweet, almost intoxicating. We were lying on the old blanket, and the grass felt dry and spiky coming through the wool. We weren't young...I mean, it wasn't a dream of our early days. We had Paul, although he wasn't there. He was still alive, though. I know, because I felt so happy, in a way I've never felt since he died.

We held each other. Your arms were around me, in the easiest way. Holding me so our chests were pressed close, but kind of loose, as if there was nothing to worry about. No one was going anywhere. You weren't afraid of losing me, and I wasn't wanting to be anywhere else. We were so free with each other.

You started to undress me. It surprised us both, and we were smiling. Grinning. It was almost funny, because we hadn't made love outside in so long, and I think we were both wondering why not. It was broad daylight, anyone could have come along, Jenny and Nat or any of the other neighbors, but we didn't care. You unbuttoned my shirt, and I undid your belt, and we pulled off our jeans. Your legs, I've always loved your legs, and then they were wrapped around me.

You know how dreams are sometimes so real, they happen in slow motion, as if to tell you it's important to pay attention, you don't want to miss anything? That's how this was. I looked into your eyes, and they were full of joy. I could tell you were seeing how much I loved you. That broke my heart, but it was a dream, so I could just rewind and feel fine again. You were caressing me, and your lips brushed mine, and I arched my back into you and I heard you whisper something.

I couldn't make out what you were saying, but you had me going, I was lost in you, completely lost. And then you said it again. The words were a little louder; I thought you said "This is how it began."

"What began?" I asked.

"You know," you said.

And I did . . . I knew. I pushed it away, because I wanted to hold on to the dream, the feeling of you making love to me. I was desperate for that. I thought, If I can just get through this, if the dream ends right, then we can still be happy. We can all be together, nothing bad will have happened.

"Make it not happen," I said to you.

"What?" you asked. "Make what not happen?"

And then I woke up.

*

I had to stop for a while, but I'm back. I'm sitting here in the kitchen, rereading your letter, wondering if you're on the way, how far you've gotten. If you're already there.

When I think about that dream, me saying "Make it not happen," there are a few things I might have meant. Isn't it strange, how the world of dreams and the world of awakening can be so different? Awake, I think I meant make Paul not to have crashed. But in the dream, I think I was talking about myself—about what I did. The two things seem to go together.

If Paul hadn't died, if I hadn't started drinking more, I wouldn't have hurt you. I know I've told you this a hundred times, nothing really happened. Nothing physical anyway. I've never been sure whether you believed me or not. I guess it's beside the point now. That snag in the sweater started long before Daniel. Just a small hole that grew between us because we didn't pay enough attention. Once the divorce is final, what will it matter? But I do find myself thinking about it.

It seems a little crazy, dwelling on it so much right now, when you're in Alaska, on your way to see where Paul died. Why am I suddenly so focused on wanting you to understand? Maybe I just think it will give us both peace at last.

What went wrong between us really had nothing to do with Daniel. He was just there. You were taking more assignments, and they all seemed to be halfway around the world, and I was lonely and crazy. I missed Paul so much, every inch of me hurt. I felt as if someone had started peeling my skin off, strips of skin down to the muscle, just turning me inside out. My nerves and blood were on the outside, and there was nothing holding me together.

You used to do that. The first days after we heard about the crash, I don't think you let go of me for one minute. You came to lie beside me after you got the call, and you put your arms around me, and I looked at your face, at your eyelashes on your cheek—that's the freeze-frame where my heart stopped. I saw the way tears were leaking out, and you didn't even have to tell me. I knew. All of it—it was as if I left my body, and you left yours, and we went flying over the whole country, into Alaska, into the bush, to see the wrecked plane, his broken body. You'll say it was just my worst fear coming true—my last words to Paul before he left about being safe, not flying in bad weather—and maybe it was.

But you held me, and I made you tell me, and that was that. I don't think we moved for hours. I couldn't breathe. I couldn't even open my eyes. I just wanted him there. I knew that if I moved even an inch, I'd have to do things. Make calls, or walk past his room, or see the postcard he'd sent us from Denali on the refrigerator. If we moved, that would make it real. So we just held each other, and that kept me together. I think it kept you together, too.

The cat finally got us up—he was hungry, and he meowed so loudly, but I barely even heard. It wasn't until he finally gave up, curled into a ball against my back, that we realized we had to feed him. Boing had been Paul's cat, after all. Poor kitty. Poor, poor little kitty. Losing Paul was hard on him, too. Do you think that's why he ran away? Because he knew Paul would never be back? Or were we as unbearable to him as we were to each other?

Sitting here in the kitchen, I can hear a very strong wind picking up outside. Cat is curled up on the top bookshelf, where the heat is rising. A storm's blowing in tonight. Storms come from the west, don't they? Did this one start in Alaska? How many days did it take to get here? Did you hear this wind, feel it buffeting your sled? If something happened to you, how would I find out? Even as I write this letter to you, I don't know where you are, what you've gone through since you last wrote me.

Anyway. I don't want to get to the rest, but I will. My dream. Daniel. What that all did to us. You, and I really don't say this to blame you, but you went away, Sam. You did that trip to Mont Blanc for *Outside*, and one to Tierra del Fuego for whomever, and then the America's Cup trials in Barcelona, and then you started talking about going surfing at Mavericks and Half Moon Bay, and that was it. It was right after that boy on his surfboard had been attacked by the white shark, and you were out to get the story. You know what I thought you were after? Suicide by shark.

You didn't know it, and I didn't know it, but I snapped. I'm tired of blaming. I felt as if I'd fallen into the Land of the Unhappy Middle-Aged Woman, spouting the catchphrases about our disappointing husbands: withdrawn, distant, emotionally unavailable. I was so sick of myself. I decided I wasn't going to tumble any further into the chasm of the pathetic.

So when the new gallery opened in town, I went down to check out the Cape Ann exhibit. I was looking for beauty, inspiration, a way to connect with everything I used to find luminous. I wanted to gaze at paintings and find truth. I'd read that there were paintings by Ruth Anderson, a woman who'd worked in Gloucester around the turn of the last century. She was an American Impressionist who'd gotten lost in the shuffle of men's reputations. I wanted to see her paintings and see if they would tell me what to do next.

I swear I wasn't looking for anything other than the chance to see another artist's work. I do remember, though, I felt like crawling out of my body. Everything hurt, the air stung my skin. You were so far away. I was hurting. I wasn't sure you loved me anymore, I didn't believe we made sense without Paul. In fact, and you must remember my screaming this at you, had we stopped loving each other even before he died? We had stopped being a couple—we were just Paul's parents, and we no longer even had him to hold us together. So what were we? There was just a huge hole where our love used to be.

So, the exhibit. I fell a little in love with Ruth. Found out most of her work was destroyed in a fire at her Boston studio. I felt that so strongly—a woman artist who'd lost so much that mattered to her. Daniel saw me standing in front of a study she'd done of dunes. Sand dunes sculpted by the wind, tufted with beach grass. Such a lonely scene. I was weeping silently. Could it be more poignant? He walked over and just stood beside me. I felt him wanting to ask me if I was okay. I was very . . . distressed.

And he finally did ask me. It was awkward. Maybe he was afraid I'd completely melt down and ruin his gallery opening. I pulled myself together and we talked about Ruth Anderson and her studio fire. At first he thought that's all it was—that I was just a supersensitive soul who cared *that* deeply about another artist's loss. I signed the guest book, put my email address down to receive notice of upcoming shows.

He wrote to thank me for coming to the opening, I wrote back to say I'd loved the show, and that's how it started. His marriage was old and dead, our marriage was . . . well, it was in trouble. On shaky ground already and grieving so badly for our son . . . Those emails made me feel alive again. You were traveling, and Daniel lived just five miles away; I'd drive by his house and see the light in his study, and know he was sitting there waiting for an email from me. That felt good.

And I'd settle down with a glass of scotch, there by the computer. I couldn't paint or draw anymore, but I could wait—that was my art in those days. The way I could sit so still, drinking single-malt scotch, vigilant for the appearance of an email. Kind of like sitting across the table from you in the old days, when I'd be drawing and you'd be writing, and the silence could stretch forever without feeling wrong. And one of us would laugh, or say something, and then the silence would come back, and it was beautiful.

So there I was, waiting. And, again not to blame you, but I wasn't hearing from you. The little "you've got mail" message was never from you. It was always from Daniel. His wife would be in the other room, watching TV or talking on the phone to one of her friends or their kids, and he'd be at the desk mooning over me. It felt good to be mooned over.

I began to get into the habit of looking forward to something. I started washing my face again. That might sound crazy to you, but it felt good to care again. Instead of just rinsing off in the shower, tilting my face up just because I had to, I'd use pretty soap. It smelled of lemons. Not that I ever thought he, Daniel, would get close enough to appreciate it—but I just felt like doing it anyway. I began caring about what I wore. I got back on my bike, and started exercising.

You'd come home between assignments, and I swear you never noticed. You'd always liked that soap, so I thought you might say something. But you didn't. We never slept close anymore. In fact, I think it was after the Half Moon Bay trip, you seemed to fall asleep on the couch more often. I began wondering if you'd started seeing someone.

Or maybe that was just my guilt. Because I was thinking about Daniel. He . . . liked me. I knew he was there for me. That sounds so dumb and tacky, but he was. He'd let me talk about Paul. You must hate that, to think of me talking about our son to someone else—but I couldn't talk about him to you. It was the one subject that was forbidden between us. The crazy thing is, I couldn't let you talk about him either. But with a stranger—it was different.

Talking to Daniel made me feel our son's presence. But then I'd wonder what he'd think about his mother getting so close to a man who wasn't his father, and I knew he'd be upset. He'd always loved the way we were together—he'd have found it impossible to believe this was happening.

When people talk about affairs, they always mean sex. Wet, sweaty, passionate, sneaking around, hard and physical. But sex isn't the most powerful part of an affair, not in the truest sense. Any two people can go to bed together. But it's the emotional attachment that counts. It's when you start preferring email with a man five miles away to talking to your husband that you know you have a problem.

*

Sorry for the disruption—the storm hit hard and knocked down a big tree. It fell on the wires outside, and I completely lost power. I tried writing you by candlelight, but it just started seeming too melodramatic, especially considering what I was saying. Besides, I couldn't find Cat for a few hours and I had to look for her. She was hiding in the yard, under the woodpile. She's so feral. My wild cat.

To skip ahead, that night when you found me and Daniel together—we were just talking. It was one of your rare periods home, and I'd found myself just feeling so frustrated. Out of my mind with it. You were there—but not really. You were absorbed with the article, writing about Mavericks, finishing up interviews with surfers and marine biologists, still trying to convince that kid who'd gotten attacked to talk to you. You were obsessed with him, with getting the story. I always thought it was because he survived. He could have died, but he didn't. Why him and not Paul? That's what I thought you were after, but you refused to talk to me about it.

I got drunk. I didn't set out to, but I never did. As you said in your last letter, it was just a little at a time. Sometimes I felt that I wasn't so much drinking the scotch as that it was drinking me. I missed Daniel—that seductive longing. It was heightened, of course, when you were home. I knew he was at the gallery—getting ready for a new show, he'd be working late. So I sent him an email, and told him I was coming over. I left the screen open. I've always figured it was just because I'd been drinking, but now I'm not sure. Maybe I wanted you to see. To know.

I walked out the door, and somehow made it into town. You noticed I was gone, and went to my computer, and you came after me. I can picture it: the gallery in that beautiful yellow Greek Revival house on Elm Street, the big windows glowing like a jewel box, lamplight silhouetting us. Our first and only real physical contact, and you were there to see us. I'm thinking of that right now, listening to the wind howl—

the storm is over, but that's how the wind is out here right now. It shrieks when it's not howling.

Sometimes I get a glimpse of myself begging you to believe me, forgive me, and I don't even know why. I think it was already over between us then, so the exercise was pointless. Daniel is still with his wife—I wouldn't be with him even if he wanted that. You can trust me on that or not, and after all this time, I guess I know how you feel.

But for what it's worth, I'm sorry. The longer I'm here, the sorrier I am. I hurt you, hurt us. If nothing else, our past together deserved better. And if there was ever any chance of fixing what was wrong between us, I gave us both a great excuse not to try.

Now, the only person I can imagine talking with about Paul is you. You're the only one who *knows*. That picture you brought . . . you say you were reaching for something out of the frame. I know what it was—Paul's Red Sox cap. You'd set the camera's self-timer, and we'd all been laughing, getting into place and trying to fit into the shot, and you'd accidentally knocked it off his head.

Paul hardly ever took it off that year—he wanted to bring luck to the team, and that was his way of doing his part. Remember how he was about the things he loved? And did he ever love anything more than the Red Sox? You and he going to those playoff games; I'm not sure he was ever happier.

Do you talk to Martha about him? Tell her about Paul? Or about us? Not you and me . . . or at least I think that's not what I mean. I mean about us as a family—we three. Then again, *do* you tell her about you and me? How could you help getting close to someone on a trip like that? Don't tell me, though. I don't want to know ...

Okay, neutral territory. Something else to write about. I went to a meeting last night. I told you about the ancient sober lobsterman—Turner. He's really wonderful. Born and raised here on Monhegan, quit drinking after he realized he was starting to love the bottle more than "his Rosie"—his wife of, as he says, a hundred years. He's full of stories and wisdom. Some of the younger guys really look up to him— for his example and discipline here, and also for everything he knows about the sea, for the life he's lived.

The season is brutal here. It's the only place in Maine— maybe in the world—where they lobster only during the harshest months, from January to June, letting the lobsters fatten up all summer. Right now, with Thanksgiving coming on, everyone is getting eager to get back to work. They talk a lot about ice and weather. It's strangely comforting to me, being among people whose daily lives incorporate the elements that killed Paul. It's as if they're fighting them for him. Or something like that ...

I found out that the man Annabelle loved was an artist by summer, lobsterman by winter. He died in a blizzard, when his boat got caught out beyond the entrance to the harbor. Annabelle was standing on the dock, calling for him—she thought he could follow the sound of her voice back to shore. It's such a touching image, and helps me understand her so much. I've been doing sketches for a painting of that storm—her on the wharf, him out at sea.

John Morgan told me the story. It turns out the reason he's here on Monhegan is that he grew up spending summers on the island and he's going through a big change in his career. He'd worked out in Seattle for a long time, doing large-scale sculptures—they'd remind you of Calder, bright works of iron, the kind you see in city parks or company courtyards. The kind you don't like. He and his wife broke up—I have no idea why, we haven't spoken about anything personal. But anyway, when he found out I was staying in this house, he told me about Annabelle.

I've asked Turner about her, too. This is the amazing thing: Annabelle's lover was Turner's brother Ralph. He was in the boat with him when he died—he said the snow was so thick and white, heavier than the fog we get here. They'd

grown up sailing these waters, and their instincts were so strong they could find their way home through any storm—until that one. He said they heard Annabelle calling over the wind, her voice guiding them in. But then they shipped a big wave, and it washed Ralph overboard. Turner tried to grab him—their hands clasped, and Turner pulled as hard as he could, but his brother just slipped away. They never found his body.

I keep seeing it all—Turner watching his brother drown, Annabelle waiting, calling, them being so close to home, almost within sight. But Ralph died. She saved Turner, but not her love. Is that the way life is, Sam?

I think of Paul saving Boing—of that entire litter, he was the only one who survived. He jumped into Paul's arms, and never really jumped out. And then, when Boing was old, Paul went to Alaska. The cat lived, but our boy died.

And I ruined everything. That's how I feel . . . I'm sorry, Sam. Those words sound so dry and old. But I mean them. I'm sorry. I talk to Annabelle and Cat about it. Cat, my little feral island stray. When you have a son who comes up with names like Boing, you just don't even try. Simple is best for me. Me and Holly Golightly. But, oh. Everything is making my heart ache. I look at Cat and think of Boing running away. So much unhappiness in our house . . .

Be safe up there, wherever you are. What are you doing for Thanksgiving? Hold tight to that photo, and promise me something? Will you kiss it for me? When you get to where Paul crashed? Kiss the picture—his face and your face. I don't want this letter to end. It's keeping me with you right now. I wish I were there.

Hadley

AURORA BOREALIS

✳ ✳

You'll wait a long, long time for anything much
To happen in heaven beyond the floats of cloud
And the Northern Lights that run like
    tingling nerves.

> —*Robert Frost* from
> "On Looking Up by Chance
> at the Constellations"

Dear Hadley—

Dogs, and wind and motion and meat and snow and trees and cold and cold and cold and dogs and darkness and tents and wet and clothes that are stiff and motion, everything in motion, and the sound of two runners in the snow and snow hooks and ganglines and more motion and sleep with your hip digging at stone and restlessness and water tasting of snow and ice and numbness.

Here are things you would want to know:

Brass does not freeze as easily as other metals, so the hooks and clips are made of brass.

Dogs can run forever. Their gait is one of the most efficient on earth.

Dogs need meat. Not suburban kibbles. They eat and they burn.

"On-by" is a command to keep going, to ignore the thing distracting you. On-by. I shout it a hundred times a day. On-by. There is a lesson somehow in on-by, but I'm not sure what it is.

You never let go of the sled. Never. If you do, the dogs will pull it away and run off. And you will be stuck in the tundra with nothing but a team of dogs to track. You do not want to be tracking dogs on foot through the bush.

Nothing about dogsledding is what you think it is. It is grunt work, mostly. It is hard and it is pushing and shoving like unjamming a car out of a snowbank. Then, when you are too exhausted to continue, it becomes easy and beautiful and you feel in harmony with every breath the dogs take. Part of you wants it to go on forever. It is all *next*. It is some sort of perfidious human desire to never be where we are, but to be next, to be the next minute forward, to escape the present. I can't adequately explain it. When you stand on the runners, you are not in one place, but in the future and the present simultaneously, and the dogs are slender backs pulling you through snow and the horizon is everything. Strange, I know. It must be what it is for you to paint. You flow into the brushes or into the picture and suddenly everything is about light and color and texture. When you look up, you are surprised to be standing in the same place. Something like that.

Hold on. I have chores.

* *

Hadley, these letters are like an old-fashioned LP and we are both standing above it, holding the stylus, trying to drop it into the start of the song. Do you remember how impossible that could sometimes be? And you occasionally put it down at the chorus, and sometimes into the opening guitar solo, or at the goofy refrain? You and I are spinning like that, within the grooves, and Paul is in there, and our house, and Boing, and the apple trees and autumn weeds and tall grass, and we are both also outside and above the plastic grooves, the stylus arm in our fingers, the needle prepared to pick up small bits and pieces of our lives. And we want to play this song, or that melody, to remember it together, but the needle has a mind of its own, doesn't it? Sometimes I see you vividly, and I experience incredible joy and contentment, and other times—yes, you with Daniel, that moment I witnessed—the needle skips and fumbles and I want to gouge out the tracks, mar the damn thing so it can never play again.

Okay, let me slow down. You must think I am a madman, and I am a little. I suspect now that part of my coming here was the hope that I could pare things down and see them once and for all—to see you every bit as much as to see Paul. I had some notions about the cold, the endless landscape, and about the simplicity of dogs, but of course nothing is simple. The dogs are pure and wonderful, but they are not simple. And running a sled across this wide, beautiful country is not what I believed it would be. I will tell you about the trip, because I know you would want to know, but first let me do a little psychological housekeeping.

First thing: I have your letters here. They arrived just before I left, almost as if fate had a hand in our affairs. I have them in my shirt pocket to keep them safe and dry. (No, not to keep them close to my heart, even I am not that corny.) I've had a strange experience reading them. In some way I don't quite understand, this fragile exchange between us seems like reality, while this trip, these dogs, the marvelous Martha, seem illusory. People always write about dreams, or about a sense of déjà vu, but I am knee-deep in it here. I want to say that I am feeling a connection to Paul, to his final moments, but that hasn't come yet. Maybe it will. I am not sure. But this other feeling, this dream feeling, is more than strange. Somehow I feel as though I have waited a life-time for this trip, that I had been destined to be here for a thousand years before, and that the dogs know I am hardly on the sled behind them. Of course I know this is a vision quest sort of thing—yes, I am that transparent—but it's also too easy, too pat to call it that. How can I make you under-stand when I hardly understand myself? I have tremendous calm right now because I know, for once in my life, that I am precisely, unerringly, uncannily, where I should be. Can you imagine what that feels like?

And here's another thing: I have dreamed of taking you every way that we have ever thought of, or dreamed of—roughly, no prisoners, with kisses that don't end, with these fierce, deep movements between us, with belts sliding off so hard they make small whip sounds, bras lifted, zippers, one leg in the pants, against walls, on tables . . . and other times, we are on a large bed, our bed, and you are entirely open to me, and it is afternoon, and the sun is working slowly away, and I am inside you, and the light is perfect, and we are so deep inside each other that nothing matters, and both of us—this is my dream, remember, my interior life right now—

both of us wonder why it isn't always like this, why we don't always stay like this when it is possible, when this sumptuous Eden is here for us, and we cast ourselves out instead of staying in this warm bed together.

We were always good together that way, Hadley. You were exciting and thrilling and sexy as hell. You just were. You are. So there.

Back to the dogs. How's that for a transition?

Okay, so here's how it has gone for me. As I told you in the last letters I sent, Gus drove me over to Martha's on our departure day. That was Thursday. When I say "drove me over" I mean, of course, that he took me on his ATV. Trucks and most vehicles are useless up here this time of year unless they can go on ice. So he drove me over. I confess I felt a bit like a boy going to his first day of summer camp. I wore some of the clothes I brought, but also an anorak that Martha gives her clients: a gray, fur-lined (caribou!) parka with a front pocket that is incredibly handy. Gloves on strings around my neck; glacier sunglasses. I looked the part even if down in my stomach I felt an imposter.

I rode behind Gus and we drove for about an hour. Not bad. The sun had just come up and the land glimmered and we saw an enormous flock of crows to the south. A murder of crows. They had found a dead moose or deer, what was left of a dead moose or deer, and they picked at skin and sinew and hair. They bent over their feed, and sometimes hopped, and they resembled men at a craps table, all hunched and intent,

67

and ready to spring away if it did not go well and ended—as it inevitably must. Gus said later that the crows are the final undertakers, short of worms. He told me about a helicopter pilot he knew who began snapping aerial photos of crows on dead things and twice he found they made patterns, and pictures, and moved like the iron filings in old Etch A Sketches to impulses we know little about. I guess they didn't compose the face of Jesus or the Virgin Mary, but they were interesting anyway. He said once they collected in the form of a picket fence, or black teeth on a white mouth, but that's as far as it went.

Martha had the sleds packed in her dooryard when we arrived. A young assistant, a teenage girl named Swahili, helped her. Swahili's parents were homesteaders—they had moved up in the late 1980s—and lived off the grid. Swahili wore dreadlocks and smelled of lavender, and was about as cool a hippie chick as you could find, but she also had tremendous competence around the dogs. I felt like the eastern dude in the cowboy movie, complete with city duds and a pen in my pocket. (Your letters, actually.) Gus knew Swahili, naturally, and they talked for a while about local gossip as they worked. They didn't intend it, of course, but my sense of being a flatlander—a newbie to this land—grew increasingly acute. I had true misgivings, wondering what in the world I was doing there. The temperature stood at about 20 degrees, but it was wet and raw and a little snow fell from time to time. Martha said the weather had a mind of its own, and the early forecast had shifted some, so she no longer anticipated an easy, routine trek. Nevertheless, she felt the time had come to go, that it wouldn't necessarily get any easier, so we started the countdown. She knew, I suspect, that psychological readiness is as important as the climate conditions.

When we were all packed, and everything checked with three run-throughs, it was time to get the dogs. Before we could do that, Martha took Swahili around the dog yard and explained which remaining dog needed medicine, which one didn't eat this or that, which one had to be kept away from the others because she had gone into estrus. Swahili knew most of it; she routinely house-sat at Martha's to care for the stay-behind dogs when Martha took out clients. For a second it felt as if Martha and I were the most mundane suburban couple about to head off to the supermarket or the local mall for a movie and dinner, leaving Swahili to babysit and that the whole thing would be concluded by midnight. But the dogs knew what was about to happen, and they went a little insane every time Martha passed among them. They wanted to go.

At last everything stood ready. I read a long time ago that sailors going out on whaling ships always felt reluctant to take the last step aboard, that they found reasons to dally that made no sense. They comprehended their fate turned the moment they committed finally to going, and I understood the full meaning of that notion at last. Here at

Martha's we were comfortable and safe. Warm quarters and food waited just a few yards away, but instead—for reasons that did not seem entirely clear, when you got down to it—we had elected to forgo comfort and chase off into the wild.

Swahili and I "lined out" our dogs, while Martha and Gus worked on the lead sled. You line out by putting the gangline on the snow—the gangline is the center line that runs straight forward from the sled and hovers between all the dogs—and then hooking the dogs in pairs down the length of the line. You dance the dogs into place by lifting their collars and letting them spring on their back legs. Most of the dogs only weigh forty pounds or so and they are elite athletes, so hopping along is a piece of cake for them. The dogs closest to the sled are wheel dogs; the dogs midway down the line run point; and the leaders, Sneak and Grabby, on my sled, run up front. We each had a ten-dog team. Martha informed me ahead of time that my dogs were not as fast or as strong as her team. I was on the junior varsity—after all these years of believing myself varsity material!—but she promised my dogs had plenty of power and stamina. And they did.

The teams stayed anchored by snow hooks. The hooks are vicious looking things, metal cobra heads with two prongs of shiny steel for fangs that jab into the snow behind the driver and attach to the harness of the sled. The harder the dogs pull, the more securely they jam the hook into the snow and ice. In theory, at least, the dogs can't go forward if one plants the snow hook properly, but Martha and Gus told me a dozen stories of snow hooks jumping out of the snow and burying themselves in mushers' legs. So, I had that to look forward to.

Anyway, I won't get too technical in these letters, but I figured you needed some of the basics. In the end, I stepped on the sled runners, watched Martha lift her hand to indicate she intended to cast off, and then I bent down and yanked the snow hook out of the ground. And I came within a fingernail's grasp of falling immediately backwards off the sled. It would have been an ignominious start, but I caught myself and the sled took off with me upright and aboard.

Understand, without Martha in front of me none of this would have occurred. I could not have simply walked up to a team and yelled "Mush" and disappeared in a cloud of snow. Imagine if you can the worst dog you ever walked on a leash, then multiply that by ten, then multiply it again by some factor that expresses the dogs' athleticism, and the fact they have been bred for centuries to do this one single thing, and you might begin to get a feeling for the enormous strength of the team. They reminded me of an undertow. Something broad and strong and inevitable.

The sled has a rudimentary foot brake and I used it a fair amount as we followed a snowmobile trail for the first few miles. The dogs, by the way, run in absolute silence. I'm not sure why I didn't know that. All their barking, their mad lunges to get going, stopped the instant we began forward.

We went from chaos—the dogs barking and jumping in the traces as high as your waist sometimes—to pure silence. It's possible, I'm told, to run a sled with two people standing on the runners, and I thought of you, Hadley, how I wanted you in front of me, my arms around you, your body leaning back into mine. Maybe we will run a team together someday. You would love that part. You would love the dogs and the silence and the trees and snow passing beside you. I've never experienced anything to match it.

We went pretty fast. World-class sprint dog teams can reach thirty miles an hour in bursts, but we ran cargo dogs and so you can picture us chugging along well under ten miles an hour. Still, that's fairly fast when you are standing on two ash 1×3s in the snow. The runners have a dimpled plastic pad where each foot belongs, so with your hands providing a third point of balance, you feel fairly stable. It required about a half hour before I began to feel I could look around at my surroundings. And about ten minutes after that, I was aware of my fingers and hands growing numb with the cold.

It's a little difficult to describe the terrain. The mountains exist off in the distance. It seems every direction you look, you see mountains. The Brooks Range. The air smells of juniper and snow and moisture. It is wet here and gullies and rivulets crisscross any trail you can find. Then the water freezes and you have heaves and buckles—nothing like it is out on the sea ice, Martha assures me—and it's like running a team over a small hedge, only the hedge is comprised of ice and is slippery as hell, and the sled invariably bounces up, then teeters down. Grunt work, as I said.

Before I forget, let me list my dog team. I already mentioned Grabby and Sneak. So it looks like this from the sled peering out over their backs.

Grabby—Sneak
Jenny—Penny (sisters)
Wiley—Dash
Blondie—Dutch
Snowball—Kya
ME

You always harness them in the same position. They prefer to run in established pairs. Occasionally Martha moves a dog up or down the line, or changes a pattern when she judges they are not running to their full potential. She works in younger dogs over the summer, but usually by the time fall arrives her lineup is set. She says it's a little like managing a baseball team, with rookies breaking in, and wily old veterans keeping the team balanced. I am, truly, running the junior varsity squad. Her dogs are faster and stronger and they break trail when it is required.

I have to stop here, sweetheart. I'm exhausted and need sleep. I'll describe the rest of the day tomorrow, if that makes sense. One thing I am thinking about right now: the last glimpses our son had of this world were as beautiful and majestic as anything that exists on this earth. Snow and whiteness and mountains and lakes that catch every reflection and mirror them so that you can sometimes forget what is the real image, and what is the light thrown back at your eyes.

Sam

November 26

To be clear, here's a note on sleeping arrangements.

We sleep in a tent. We sleep in fat clothes, with our hoods pulled up and a small stove operating in the center of the tent. If any dog has come up lame, or has a problem, the dog sleeps inside the tent with us. Grabby, my newest girlfriend, sleeps next to me. She is a little old, I guess, and Martha dotes on her. Sneak also sleeps inside. The rest of the dogs sleep on a line outside the tent. Martha circles the tent with the dogs—a precaution against bears, she told me, and yes, we have a shotgun with us for moose and potentially bears— and they burrow into the snow. The inside tent temperature is usually around 45. We smell of food and dogs and lamp oil. We do not bathe, by the way, until we return. Martha has taught me to wash my hands in tea water—everything is used, and reused—and we are frugal in the extreme. The tent has a small hole at the top to let our heat and breath escape, and lying next to Grabby—a sweet, thirty-five-pound female with a curled tail and one black paw, who uses her nose like dolphins use their noses on TV shows, constantly flipping it to get you to pay attention or to keep rubbing her—I can usually see out at the stars and the black night.

Sleeping in a tent up here is many things, but it is not exactly the circumstances for the man-woman thing, I promise.

That cozy island life you're living would seem a much more likely setting.

It turns out she is from Massachusetts, of all places. I don't know why, but that makes me laugh. I suppose I thought of her as a mountain woman, born on a bearskin in a hut at the North Pole somewhere, but she grew up in the suburbs outside of Boston and is a die-hard Red Sox fan. (Paul would like that.) She moved here with a geology expedition—an oil company thing, actually, for Exxon, I think—and then fell in love with the territory. She made a good salary as an engineer and she bought a hundred acres and then slowly built her place. The dogs came by accident, mostly. An old-timer died and left about a dozen sled dogs and no one wanted to bother with them, so the police had plans to shoot them, then Martha heard about it and intervened. She said the last thing in the world she wanted, or thought about, was sled dogs. But when she agreed to take them on, the police passed along a few sleds that had been around the cabin, and an old trapper named Jim—a friend of the old guy who died—helped her set up her first dog yard and taught her the basics. After that, she said, it was like anything else: you started as an amateur and became more competent. She tapped into a dogsledding community little by little and the rest is history, as the saying goes.

Martha is smart. I suspect her wisdom has come from shaking out of many of our usual life commitments. She is committed to the dogs, true, but she spends almost no time on what most people in modern life do to occupy themselves. No trips to the mall, or the grocery store—except about four times a year—and no sitting at stoplights or driving mindless errands in a car. All of that energy we use for everyday routines is channeled elsewhere in her life. It feels almost as though she has a reservoir other people don't possess—that she is not as scattered and drawn as most Americans. Anyway, I'd like you to meet her someday. As one gets older, it feels harder and rarer to be impressed by another human being, but she impresses me.

She said one thing you might find illuminating regarding Paul's adventures up here. She said she has come to believe every person alive is part snake, and she contends people have to shed their skin as surely as a snake does in order to grow. She said you can never tell when a person needs to molt. Some do it early on, some late. Some do it a couple times during a life, but she says everyone will do it at least once. She said Paul's heading up to the north country to work was his first transformation. She said he would have come back changed in unexpected ways, stronger maybe, weaker maybe, but different. She said we cannot blame ourselves for what happened, because Paul needed to grow, plain and simple, and that you cannot prevent a person from cracking the casing that has held them. They have to go through it, that's all, and she claims she changed when she moved up here. Who knows why? She had a good job, a comfortable life, and then she chucked it to run dogs and lead expeditions. She doesn't make nearly the money she once did, but her days belong to her, and she believes, but doesn't know for certain, that she is finished molting.

All this discussion of change, Hadley, makes me wonder what we are doing. You and me. It feels entirely natural to be in contact with you, but I don't want to skip over the distance between us. I love you, Hadley, and always will, but I understand we have changed, too. I don't want either of us to rush, or to discount the days that have passed between us. I am open to you, but I am not entirely the same husband I was before Paul's death. You are not the same wife. In the excitement of receiving your letters, I don't want to cheapen the profound changes we have both undergone. We are not schoolkids with crushes. You are my wife. If I have jumped too quickly to assumptions, or hurried too fast along a track, I apologize. I don't know if Martha is correct about peoples' need to molt, but something has changed with us. I recognize that. I know you do, too. It makes no sense to name it, though. Not yet. I trust these letters.

Sam

Hadley—

This is the third day. I skipped a day because I was too exhausted to write. I am bone tired, but otherwise in good spirits. This morning we saw our first moose, an enormous creature with a rack as wide as a Volkswagen. It trotted through our camp and Martha hurried to shush the dogs. I guess the moose are in rut and any noise or irritation can turn them surly. Moose are a bigger problem than bears when you are running dogs, she said, although polar bears on some expeditions are a true menace. She said a basic grizzly will follow a camp sometimes, and even look for opportunities to steal food, but for the most part they are wary of humans and stand clear. Polar bears, on the other hand, hunt everything. They live on such a thin margin that they cannot afford to pass up an opportunity of any kind. Martha has a friend who came north to photograph the landscape and ptarmigan for *National Geographic*. A German guy. He was transported way up on Baffin Island and he went to bed in his tent with a shotgun beside him. He had posted a laser trip wire around his tent so that anything passing closer would trigger an alarm, but the bear stepped over it like a cat burglar, and the German fellow woke up to feel himself being slowly dragged out of his tent by the foot of his sleeping bag. No sound. That's what the German found most remarkable. The entire episode had taken place without as much as a broken stick. Fortunately the German reached back and was able to grab his shotgun—by the hair on his chinny chin chin the way Martha described it—and then swung the barrel around and put it against the bear's forehead. He said even as he did it the bear did not pounce or do anything aggressive or ferocious. It reminded him, he said, of a well-trained dog sliding a piece of bacon off the kitchen table. The bear didn't want to do it, he knew he shouldn't do it, but that bacon was too hard to resist.

Bear stories. Not as good as shark stories, but they have their moments. The German pulled the trigger and the blast peeled the bear back in two sections and dropped it dead.

Okay, I need to say something. It's about Daniel and what I saw that night and what it did to me. I don't know why, but I am haunted by the evening more than anything else I can call to mind. You and Daniel. Daniel and you. And his hands.

First, I want to acknowledge every last thing you said. Yes, I was distant. Yes, I had deliberately taken assignments that forced me away from the house. And, yes, Paul's death—how in the world can we even calculate that into the equation? I took you for granted. I did. I know that. In the devastated state I knew myself to be in, you felt—please try to understand this—like a chore. You were one more thing to do, one more thing to factor in when I had no desire to think of anyone but myself. Selfish, I know, but human, I would argue. We have talked about Paul a thousand times, but how can we ever fully comprehend what his death meant? How can we ever swallow that last full spoonful of utter loss? Hell, I am halfway across Alaska on a dogsled, still chasing something about Paul that we know can't be captured. So perhaps we just have to accept Paul's death as a prime mover, something that pushes us in directions we can't always explain. I couldn't be with you. Not for daily chats, not for a cocktail, not for a should-we-clean-up-the-garden-and-spread-compost-on-it kind of married discussion. To have engaged in that kind of conversation would have killed me or driven me mad right then. So, true, I had no psychological room to rent.

I'll add this. I took a certain delight in not being available to you. There, I've said it. I felt you blamed me for Paul's death. Intellectually we both understood it was an accident, a horrible twist, but I felt in your bones you believed I had pushed Paul to take on an adventure like this. Though you never said it, I perceived a haze of blame, a motherly accusation that the older male had been unfair to the young male, your son. I understand that if I pinned you down this second, or if I said it to you face to face, you would deny it. And maybe part of you will deny it even reading it here. But I believed it to be true, felt it in my heart, and used my absence as a way to get back at you for such a terrible accusation.

Now you know. I don't know if a thing like this can be shaven and cleaned and made to live between us. I don't know. But now you understand why I did not stay near you, why I accepted assignments to get me out of the house. Not noble, but perhaps forgivably male. I'll let you decide.

Now Daniel.

I hate the bastard. Is that too blunt and unexamined? I hate his guts, everything he stands for, the pretense to art, his little "jewel-box windows," as you call it, his appeal to the women of the town, his lurking, especially his lurking, on the computer, waiting to talk to you, his wife in the other room. I hate him for that. And I hated you for falling for it. You were too smart to fall for it, too smart to give in even in a small way to that jerk. I understand, I do, that you also went nearly insane after Paul's death. I know that I had made myself unavailable to you. But Daniel? Good grief. He was such a cliché. I would have had more respect for your misstep if it had been with a local construction guy, or a cop, or almost anything. Sorry. I am not blaming you a second time, but if these letters mean anything, we might as well be honest.

So, yes, when I saw what you had written in your email to him, when I knew you had gone to town to see him, I felt a deep, horrible train running through my stomach. Call it an excruciating nightmare when you know you shouldn't look, you shouldn't turn to see what has slithered up the stairs, but you have to turn anyway and put your eyes on the horror that came at least partially from your own imagination.

I parked across the street. I watched you. Here's a thing I never told you. Part of me, a sliver of me, accepted the pain of seeing you in another man's arms. Does that sound per-verse? I'll tell you why I felt that way. I saw you, Hadley. It felt like a slap across my face, like the world sending me a message, and when he slid his hand off your waist and put it on your hip, ready to move down—the greedy bastard—I saw you as the girl I had fallen in love with, the woman I had loved for years, and you were no longer part of me, no longer a married woman, but Hadley Emmet, the beautiful woman on a bicycle I had fallen for the instant I saw her. You were free again. You lived apart from me, and all the pain of Paul's death, all the pain we had caused each other—suddenly it disappeared for a flicker and I saw you. Just you. And you turned a little, and your hair swung out, and your shoulder tucked in, and I knew that gesture, knew it so deep in my tis-sue that I could hardly breathe. It was not a married woman making that gesture, not a wife, giving herself to Daniel. It was you, the core of you, and I hated you for it, and I forgave you for it even as I despised what I saw.

Then we had our big scene, didn't we? The loud voices, the angry words. Another cliché. It is so clear now that Daniel was merely a symptom of the trouble between us, not a true threat, but my male ego had been punctured. It had. I saw, too, that for a moment at least, you wanted him. I've al-ways loved your hunger, and to see it turned for an instant on another man nearly derailed me once and for all. So we fought. Made a scene. Then, of course, I had carte blanche to take any assignment I liked. I puffed up with righteous indignation, though I would have put it some other way to myself. Time apart. Breathing space. All those lousy terms we use to protect ourselves. Daniel was fuel. That's all.

If he's back with his wife, hooray for him. Too bad for her. I am not going to promise I will ever put Daniel out of my thoughts. He will stay there, a little grit of sand. Sorry, but he will. But I can live with the discomfort as long as I know he is out of your life.

I've gone on too long. Enough for now. I feel wrung out and tired as I have seldom been tired. Martha said we might run into a snowmobile crew or two somewhere in the next day, so if we do, I'll ask them to carry this to the lodge and mail it. I am thinking of you right now, Hadley. The real you, the heart of you. Daniel never touched her, not my Hadley.

Sam

Hadley—

Okay, to lighten up. A conversation you would enjoy, entirely off subject. Picture it late at night, dogs snoring, cold wind blowing, Martha flat on her back, me flat on my back, the hiss of the stove now and then. Cold in the tent, maybe 40, but warm in the sleeping bag. Kind of like a junior high sleep-out, only warped up by a factor of eighty. Martha's voice is a little scratchy, like a kid talking through an oscillating fan.

Me: So were you ever married?

M: Once, but it didn't take.

Me: How long?

M: Six months. He proposed to me at a Celtics game and they posted my response on the scoreboard. I thought it was incredibly romantic, but looking back it feels slightly insane. Why do Americans think public proposals are so charming?

Me: Did they put your picture on the scoreboard?

M: Yes. And the strange thing is, we got married because our pictures had been put up there. Doesn't that beat all? We both knew we weren't well matched, but we had done this incredibly public thing, broadcast to the entire Celtics audience around New England, and both our families saw it. He had called my mother and father and they had started up the whole phone chain. So when I said yes, and they flashed our picture on the video board, it was like we had signed a contract to marry or die.

Me: And you knew it wasn't right?

M: We both knew it as we were doing it! (One of the few times I have heard Martha raise her voice. It made me laugh and the dogs raised their heads and looked around.) That's what made it nutty. It was as if we had to walk to our execution while knowing we could stop it at any time if we simply dug our heels in. But we had been recorded at the Celtics game!

Me: You still a Celtics fan?

M: Hate them. (getting sleepy)

Me: That's too bad.

M: What they should do, they should make couples who divorce after these big public proposals—they should have to come back to the Celtics game and admit they got divorced. You know, hold up the divorce decree so the Celtics fans can see that. That would be better drama.

There, a little taste of Martha. Even the noble, dog-driving, north woods woman has endured her humiliating moments. Love levels us all. It is nearly incomprehensible to imagine Martha at a Celtics game with a big grin on the Mega-tron (or whatever they call the scoreboard) and her attentive beau beside her. But there she was.

We heard snowmobiles late last night, and Martha says we may strike a trail later this morning. I will pass these letters along and hope they find their way to you. I am thinking of

Paul right now. He was a fine boy, sweetheart. If we never did anything else but create such a fine human being—better than us both, I think—then our lives would still be well spent. I miss him so.

Sam

Dear Sam,

On-by. You're right—there's something to be learned in that. It expresses a sort of letting go, detachment. I'm not there yet. But I like the phrase . . .

Thanksgiving was hard. I missed you and Paul so much. I remember how when he was little, he'd come home from school on Wednesday—they always had a half day. And I'd be baking the pies, and doing the things my mother always did for holidays—polishing the silver, making cranberry sauce, fixing creamed onions, only those things always seemed to come so naturally to her, and I was always worried I couldn't measure up, and he would help me. He was so sweet, Sam. When he was in first grade, I'd pull a chair over to the sink for him to stand on, and he'd just do whatever I gave him . . . He always liked helping and he loved polishing the silver, seeing the tarnish coming right off before his eyes. Instant gratification.

This year I didn't even want to notice the day. The weather has been so cold, with snow falling almost every night. I've been feeling like a hibernating bear—pulling the covers up over my head and waiting till the spring thaw. The nights get dark so early, it's easy to hide. The island is pretty deserted right now, except for the lobster fishermen getting ready for their season and a few stragglers like me. Cat keeps me company, but she still won't let me pet her.

Turner actually came and knocked on my door, told me the church was having a turkey dinner for the AAs. It was the last thing I felt like doing, but I made myself. And in a funny way, I'm glad I did. There was a meeting first, and the topic— perfect for Thanksgiving—was "gratitude."

It's been hard for me to feel grateful for much. No matter how clear the sky, or how bright the morning, or how warm the fire, none of it has mattered much in light of losing Paul. And—I'm glad this is a letter so you can't interrupt me— losing you. I never thought that would happen.

Your letters have stirred me up, especially the—well, the hard parts. The part about Daniel, to be exact. Sam, I knew you felt it—it was obvious, the way you couldn't stand to look at me, meet my eyes. Would things between us have turned out differently if we'd faced this before you moved out? Maybe it's only possible to do it in letters. Reading your words, I hear your voice, and I'm almost glad I don't have to look into your face. It's terrible to realize what I did to you, to us. What I broke. I appreciate your taking part of the blame, not that blame is the point.

What is the point? Understanding, maybe. On-by.

From the very beginning, I knew we belonged together. I'd never known how lonely I was until I fell in love with you. I'd lie beside you and feel you were part of me but somehow not, too, somehow so exotic and unknowable, and I'd feel I could look into your eyes forever, just touching you and caressing your face, your beard, and the way it felt to my hand, and the way my heart would feel as if it was beating outside my rib cage, and we'd just gaze at each other and you'd never look away first. I loved you for that . . .

I felt such passion for you. I couldn't sleep when you were away from me, and I couldn't sleep when you were right there. I felt this huge worry—I could never put it into words, but it felt as if my being couldn't support such emotion. My body, my spirit, I was afraid I couldn't handle the intensity. I had never felt so close to anyone, but I wanted even more than what we had—honestly, I think I wanted to be right inside your skin with you.

Because that's the only way I could hold you for sure. When you went away on assignment, and I mean even early on, before Paul died, I used to imagine you meeting gorgeous, amazing, athletic younger women—and as much as you assured me both that you *did* and that they didn't matter to you, it took me years to get comfortable with that reality. I finally began to trust you—even more, trust us, you and me . . . I wasn't so much like a howling dog anymore, but one who had circled and circled and finally come to rest.

And it got to the point that even when you were gone, I felt you with me. We knew each other so well—that was part of it. You'd say a word and I could finish your thought. You'd touch me, and I'd lean in for more. When you were gone, I'd feel you in bed beside me. And I'd take a walk through the orchard, and I'd hear you egging me on, to climb a tree. I wanted you as much as at the beginning, but gradually I felt safer. You never broke a promise to me, and that counted so much.

All these thoughts swirling around—to have loved you so much, and now to be on opposite sides of the world with the divorce proceeding, and to receive these letters from you, so full of the voice of my husband Sam, yet also full of . . . it feels like a new life. Your description of the trip is thrilling, and I feel very far away from you.

So going back to Thanksgiving dinner and gratitude as a topic at the meeting—I was really torn, didn't want to go. But Turner dragged me there—tall, stooped, taciturn Yankee that he is—he reminded me that the holidays are the Bermuda Triangle for alcoholics, a time a lot of us start drinking again, and forced me to sit in the front row of the church hall. And (I can truly see you cringing at the thought of this next part, "sharing" feelings with a roomful of strangers) when we went around the room, and everyone was saying

what they felt thankful for—"sobriety," "my family," "my new boat," "a good report from the oncologist," and when the circle came round to me, I said "Sam's letters."

And it's true. I'm thankful we're back in touch. In fact, sitting here in the cottage with a fire crackling and fine sleet pelting the windows, I've just reread your last letters and can almost, almost pretend you're right here. Remember when we were together, what a chore it was to get me to go out? I never saw the point of going to parties, or the movies, or the repertory theater when I could just be home alone with you . . .

So here we are. Sam and Hadley.

So much in your last letters to talk about . . . Martha—as wonderful as she no doubt is—is like a toothache to me; you know how when you have a cavity, and you can't stop touching it with your tongue, to see if it's still there and as bad as you thought? Well, that's how I feel about her. And yes, what right do I have to even care, etc. etc. etc.?

You said she's smart, and I know how much you like smart people, how swayed you can be by intellect. Not only that, but I read what you wrote and realize I would like her. She sounds great. The part about her saving that team of sled dogs—I love her for it, and you can tell her that. And the fact she bought a hundred acres all by herself, found a way to live on them—if you tell me she has solar panels and is trying for a zero energy footprint (and she sounds like someone who probably does) I'll love her even more.

That might be why I'm having such a hard time imagining you in such close quarters with her. Because she's just the kind of person you would love, too.

You tell me what she said about shedding skin. Of course that's one part of what Paul was doing. I'm not sure we needed her to tell us that. He couldn't grow and change anymore here at home, because we loved him too much—even being at college he knew we would have done anything for him, and he had to chafe at us, escape from us. Had to drop out of Amherst and upset us, had to rebel, had even to leave Julie, had to fly thousands of miles away. She's right about that.

But did you tell her how thrilled he was to be accepted into Amherst in the first place? Early decision—that was a strong commitment. Do you remember those months before he applied, when the dining room table was given over entirely to his college essays? Just piles of books and applications and financial forms, and how hard he worked on them all? I'd stand in the kitchen looking at the back of his head, at his messy brown hair, seeing him hunched over writing, and my stomach would hurt because I was so afraid he'd be disappointed. That he wouldn't get into Amherst.

But he did. I think about it now—how over the moon he was, and I'll never understand, not really, why he didn't go back. I know what he told us, about wanting to teach Inuits and help the village—you know I've never believed that was all there was to it. I'm sure he was telling the truth about why he wanted to go there—but that came after, didn't it? Chronologically wouldn't he have first had to decide he wasn't returning to college? Did something go wrong that he couldn't tell us? I know it wasn't anything to do with Julie—she would have told me. What made him not go back to the college he'd strived to get into early decision, worked so hard for?

I'm thinking of that class he took—LJST. Law, Jurisprudence, and Social Thought...not that he ever would have been a lawyer, but he loved Professor Dunlop, said he changed the way he thought. And I asked Paul once what was so important about that class. He told me they'd had to read Hemingway's "Hills Like White Elephants." And I'd read it, and forgotten it, but Paul asked me if I knew what it was about. I thought I did, but he told me—and I didn't. It was about abortion, even though it's never mentioned, not even once.

The class had read the story, and they thought it meant one thing, but Professor Dunlop had them stop, and read that part where the girl says, "And you think then we'll be all right and happy?" And the boy says, "I know we will. You don't have to be afraid. I've known lots of people who have done it." "So have I," said the girl. "And afterwards they were all so happy."

And Paul said they wouldn't necessarily have realized what it was about, or that the girl was being sarcastic, if the professor hadn't made them stop and think. The class taught him to look more deeply, that what might seem one way on the surface can be something else entirely down below. People can seem to be talking about one thing when it's not that at all, it's something unspoken and maybe even unknown. And he said that gave him a new and completely different way of thinking about life, the ways people interact, the subversive ways we try to persuade people of our points of view.

So does Martha think Amherst—his real and true dream, and those classes he felt were teaching him how to think about the world and justice and art and looking deeply and the green hills of Africa, not to mention Julie—was part of what he needed to shed? You can tell I'm not really resting easy with her theory.

As a matter of fact, I don't like the snake image. You know I've always had a viper thing—used to make you tell me stories about the snakes you saw in Australia and Africa. Snakes and sharks, why do I love you to tell me about creatures that scare me the most? So that bothers me a little, you talking snakes with her.

Do you remember that book by Madeleine L'Engle? *A Wind in the Door*? It came after *A Wrinkle in Time*, and Paul loved it. He loved that it was about a family where the father traveled (you) and the mother stayed home (me) and the children were smart, wry, and unsentimental (him). He loved the fact Meg and Charles Wallace and their twin brothers had a pet snake—Louise. Because anyone could love a cute kitten or puppy, but most people balk at reptiles. Paul was always the champion of the unlovable, the unappreciated. I swear the reason he loved that book so much was that Louise the snake helped save the dying little boy. He had such a good heart, didn't he? He didn't distinguish between creatures with fur and those with scales.

Oh, I miss him. Writing about him brings him back. His spirit, his essence, a flash of memory, the sound of his voice. But it's all so inadequate, compared with the real thing, with my living son. If I could have him with me for one more hour, what would I do? Cut off my arm, certainly. Give my life. I would do that, if I could see Paul again.

We gave our marriage. You realize that, don't you? Losing Paul made it impossible for us to exist. He died, and we became ghosts. I can sit here and examine what happened. Daniel, my drinking, you disappearing on assignment and even when you were home. But that's just any old long marriage. People get tired—of their lives, themselves, each other. When a child dies, though, that's another story. That's the sky being torn and the earth's crust being rent, a new plague that affects only your family, and knowing that until you yourself die, every minute will be filled with agony. I was shocked to realize this excruciating pain was made worse by looking into your eyes. Not just because you and he have/had the same eyes, although there is that—but because you gazed upon him as he came out of my womb, took him from the doctor and held him before anyone else, handed him to me. So after the plane crash, when I looked into your sad, hollow eyes, I saw the reflection of that moment and so many that followed. I saw our boy's life, and that life is no more. And I just couldn't stand it. It made me, forgive me, unable to look at you.

Enough. I never want to talk about this again.

* *

I'm back. After I wrote that part about kittens and puppies, I realized I hadn't seen Cat in a few hours. She's so skittish and feral, and she can hide so completely, days can go by without my seeing her. But the weather is brutal right now, and I wanted to make sure she hadn't slipped out through one of the cracks.

She was curled up in my sweater drawer. I've gotten to know her favorite places, like under the quilt on my bed, so flattened against the mattress no one would ever guess she was there. And, when I'm not burning wood in the fireplace, she likes to jump up into the chimney and hide on the smoke shelf. I always have to look up into the flue with a flashlight before starting the fire to make sure she's not there. The other day I shined the beam up into the stone chimney, and there were two yellow eyes glowing down at me.

She's lying beside me now, curled up under the covers, just out of reach of my feet. She likes to be close, but she doesn't like me to touch her. I'm writing this from bed, because it's bone-chillingly cold and damp, and because I'm imagining you in Alaska where it's probably three times colder than this. Do you remember how I used to feel what you were feeling? It was spooky, but when you were near the equator I'd get a fever, and when you went north or far south, when you were near the poles, I'd start shivering and have to put on a sweater.

Something strange is happening to me. I have your letters here, and I want to go through them point by point, answer everything you said about Daniel, lob some more defensive strikes at Martha. I'm tempted to tell you that I had coffee with John Morgan just to get a rise out of you. The truth is, I did, but all he wanted to talk about was his sculpture and the big one-man show he's having in the spring. He's split with his wife, and there's someone else—a beautiful grad student he met at, of all places, Clyde Lorus's villa in Greece. Clyde collects his work or something, and the grad student was there with a boyfriend who's signed to whatever the hell record label Clyde Lorus is connected with, I should know but I don't, and John stole the grad student right from the hot young rocker, and John's wife is depressed and calls him crying and can't talk except to whisper she wants him back, wants their marriage back, and he doesn't know what to do, he's stopped caring about that part of his life, he can only think about when he's going to see Lyra—that's the grad student's name—again, because he's worried she might go back to the hot young rocker, but he has to stay here and finish his work for the big spring show. I sat silently and listened and felt a little sick. How stupid we all are.

What you wrote about Daniel is haunting me, because now I see what you saw.

There's a poem by Mary Oliver, "Wild Geese," that goes, "You do not have to be good / You do not have to walk on your knees for a hundred miles through the desert, repenting." But I feel as if I did have to do that, repent. My knees are rubbed raw. I've felt so terrible and guilty. I'm not sure that I've come to Monhegan exactly to forgive myself—I think I'm just too tired to keep doing this.

I'm really tired. So I'm going to stop.

I think I'm beginning to really get the hang of on-by...

You're turning me into a Buddhist, my darling. I read something by the Dalai Lama on the Diamond Cutter Sutra and seventy verses on emptiness. He speaks of the scope of suffering. I think he might have been writing about parents who've lost children. Is that the ultimate emptiness? I know it's the ultimate suffering.

Hadley

Hi Sam,

It's twenty-four hours since I stopped mid-letter, and all I can say is the sun is out. Bright, shining sunlight hitting the rocks and harbor all day long, moving across the island, making it warm enough to sketch outside, at least for brief periods. The wind is strong and steady, but I've been drawing in the lee of some granite boulders. I'm enclosing some of the sketches here so you can get an idea of the landscape.

Cathedral Woods is so thick with tall pines, almost no sunlight penetrates—but neither does snow nor strong gusts of wind. It's eerie, with boughs creaking and the air whistling through the pine needles at the very tops of the trees. This morning I walked through on my way to the lee shore, and I really understood why they named it as they did. I was all alone—not another human being around; the sound of my boots walking across the soft bed of pine needles made me feel I was the only one on the entire island. But I felt a presence—a warmth inside and a sense that I was surrounded by goodness. I had to stop, try to hold on to the feeling—and I wished you were there. It reminded me of how nature was always our church, yours, mine, and Paul's, how mystical and sacred the outdoors always felt to us.

Down a sloping hill I found a small hollow, dug out between boulders and looking over a series of rocky inlets. The coastline is jagged and treacherous, with waves crashing and churning, salt spray shooting into the sky. It's impossible to imagine anything surviving that wave action, yet the coves are full of seals. They sunbathe on the rocks, which ice over between tides—and they curve, snout and tail upward, just like bananas. Then they dive and glide, and ride the cold frothy waves, their heads poking up to watch me draw them, their eyes so black and bright.

And there are shorebirds, too: harlequin ducks, common eiders, white-winged scoters, surf scoters, long-tailed ducks, alcids, and black-legged kittiwakes. Yesterday I saw what looked like a soccer ball washed up on the seaweed above the tide line, and it was a snowy owl. And all I could think of was, you must have them up there, too—you're close to the tundra, and that's their natural habitat.

You mentioned the moose and the bear, and even the polar bear and the German, and now you have me worried about you being attacked by beasts. Here on Monhegan there is no dangerous game—other than sharks in the sea, just birds and squirrels and deer and raccoon. (I'm collecting a series of delicious shark stories for you, one involving Turner baiting his lobster pots when he heard a great breath, almost like a whale or a dolphin coming up for air, and when he turned to look, he saw a great white shark with its entire head poking up out of the calm sea, trying to get a peek over the gunwale of his lobster boat, to see what morsels he could steal...)

And islanders. There's a camaraderie that exists here just by nature of living so far at sea in so few square miles. When I walk back toward town from the inlet, I see smoke wisping out of chimneys and feel a kind of coziness and homecoming, as if I'm somewhere I belong. The town is tiny, just a street and a general store and a post office and the ferry dock. There's the Island Inn overlooking the harbor and uninhabited Manana Island, and the sunsets, and there's a tiny library.

Now that I'm officially a year-rounder (at least this year) they've told me the big secret—Jamie Wyeth doesn't live here anymore! The myth of Jamie looms large over the summer art community. People really do make pilgrimages here to connect with the Wyeth mystique. I'm not sure whether they're afraid that if tourists find out they wouldn't come, or whether—and I think this is more like it—they enjoy the joke. But the truth is, there's an austerity to the beauty here that reminds me so much more of Andrew Wyeth, Jamie's father.

That subtle palette he always used, shades of wheat and gray, white and cream. Voile curtains at the window, weather-beaten barns, salt-silvered shingles. When I used to visit my aunt in Hartford, she'd take me to the Wadsworth Atheneum, and my favorite painting was by Andrew Wyeth, of a house on the coast; it was painted from the perspective of the wood-shingled roof, looking past a lightning rod with a pale-yellow glass ball pierced by the needle, and the late-year beach and sea spreading out behind and below in the distance.

The canvas was so simple, so not showy. His brushstrokes were fine, almost invisible. He used gouache, the first time I took note of that as a medium. The painting had the sense of a photograph, very fine and precise, the view neither added onto nor subtracted from but simply rendered, not exactly black and white but delicately colored, almost as if time and memory had bleached it of any rich or strong hues. The feeling was pure November—clear light, a sort of sadness, a moment of reflection. I loved it.

That's what Monhegan feels like to me: that painting, my favorite by Andrew Wyeth. No matter that the seasons will pass, there's a November quality to this island. Summer is over, the prettiest part of fall has gone by—there are no bright yellows, no sugar maple reds, no flowers left. Christmas is still to come—no lights yet, or trees, or wreaths or decorations. There's no artificial cheer. Everything is brown, gray, black, white, and dark, dark forest green. It suits the way I feel, and it's beautiful.

I've rented the house through May—and I know I said I wanted to buy it, sell our house and stay here, and maybe I still will. But after all my enthusiasm in the first few letters, I'm suddenly not sure. This might sound crazy, but I feel

I was meant to come here for right now, this very winter. But equally, I feel as if perhaps I'm not meant to stay. Annabelle has been silent lately, leaving me alone with my thoughts.

I feel very in-between right now.

Two nights ago I had another dream. I won't give you all the details ... I can't understand them myself. But I know I was on the sunporch at home, and the feeling that you were there, too, in another part of the house, was very strong. I heard your footsteps coming up behind me, and closed my eyes to wait for you to hold me, and then I woke up.

Did you know the part of the brain that dreams is very old? I get this mixed up, but I'll try. There's the front part of the brain, the midbrain, and the hindbrain. The midbrain is where dreams and emotions occur. The limbic system. The front part is where reason and logic happen—things that only humans have, while the midbrain is closer to an animal's—it's almost primitive. That's why dreams are so illogical ... because they take place in the less developed part of the brain, where there's less order and ordering.

I'm sitting with Cat—she's right on the arm of the chair beside me—and thinking of you with Grabby and Sneak and the other dogs, and I know you know how alike them we are. Animals aren't burdened with reason; they don't have to think about whether they like or trust someone, whether a person is good or bad—their instincts just take over and tell them how they feel. And they know what they know and don't second-guess themselves.

You know what I'm realizing? I don't know what I want. I feel I'm on this island so far out in the Atlantic, separated, in some ways, from life. There was before Monhegan, and someday there'll be after. What will "after" look like? I have no idea. I thought I knew something of what I wanted—to start painting again. That's happening, but now what? There has to be more.

Doesn't there?

This is where the animals have it easier. They don't ask such questions. They just live. . . .

Hadley

Dear Sam,

If my writing looks strange, forgive it. Yesterday I slipped on the ice and cracked my right wrist. My drawing hand is all swollen and bruised. It's hard to write, but I wanted to tell you. Also—this is awful to say—they gave me some pain pills at the clinic, and I took one. Am I still sober if I take a Vicodin? Some people in the program would say no.

I was across the island, on those rocks I love so much. The sun was out, and it was late afternoon. Shadows had stretched over the land, and I was cold, but I couldn't leave—it was a pure moment, with sun and shade and the light changing so slowly, thin sun coming through a veil of clouds that had an aspect of parchment, this lovely obscured yellowed-ivory light.

Finally I was shivering so much I couldn't hold the pencil anymore, so I stood up to leave. And that was all—I took half a step and my heel hit some ice, and my feet just flew out from under me. I landed right on my side, and when I stuck my hand out to brace my fall, I really banged it. It's not broken, though.

Can you believe it? Sam, I was so scared. I landed flat on the rocks, and the pain was so intense I passed out. I've never broken anything before. I know you have, and of course there was the time Paul broke his leg at Mad River. So when

I came to, that's what I thought had happened—that I'd broken my leg like Paul, and that I'd have to lie there and wait for help. I thought maybe I'd freeze there and die. But I didn't—I was fine, or almost fine.

It was almost dark when I fell, and by the time I dragged myself home, it was pitch-black. I heard Cat meowing as I came down the street; it sounded as if she was crying, and that made me cry, too. Not for me, but . . . oh, Sam. I don't even want to write this, but if I don't ask you, I'll go crazy.

Do you think Paul was hurt? I mean, did he feel pain before he died? I've never had the courage to voice this until now, and I can't bear to think it, but I have to know. Don't hide anything from me. When I fell there on the rocks, I went out so fast. I almost didn't know what happened. But when I came to—oh, Sam, I knew instantly. I felt the pain, and saw the purple shadows on the water, saw little dots of light, the kind you see when you're just passing out, because I hurt so much—and I wasn't sure I could move. I just thought of Paul, those last minutes. What were his like, his last minutes?

This is what I don't want to think—I don't even want to write it. Sam, did he know the plane was crashing? Did he feel himself falling out of the sky? You said it was ice on the wings, making the plane too heavy. So that means it wasn't sudden, right? There was time to think and react.

It means he knew what was coming, that's what I don't want to hear but have to know. Just tell me. Please, as soon as you can. Even though I'm not sure I can stand to hear it. I read a book once that said when planes crash and the black box picks up the last words of the pilots and anyone in the cockpit, they're heard calling for their mothers. That's what's killing me, Sam—the idea that Paul died calling for me.

Julie is coming out here. She and I always like to see each other during the holidays, so she's taking the ferry out from Port Clyde next week. I'm not prepared for her this year. Three years now and suddenly it seems harder than ever.

And that question I asked in my last letter—what do I want? How does it all add up? The painkiller has a strange side effect; it keeps me from being able to block out thoughts. I can't censor or stem what's coming up. I'm getting an answer I never thought I'd get. Chalk it up to the Vicodin, maybe...

I'm sending this to the most recent address you gave me—Laika Star—and don't know when you'll get it. Be careful, Sam. Life is dangerous.

Hadley

Hadley—

I'm back. Does that surprise you? Time is different for people when they are separated. I am back and I am safe and I have been to Paul's last moment. I have a great deal to report.

I am not feeling well, Hadley. I considered not telling you, but I know how you would be if you found out I kept it from you. I have pneumonia by most accounts. I guess it settled into my lungs on the trip and I was not well for the return. I made it, though. We have been snowed in since just after we arrived back, so I have not been able to see a doctor. Gus, believe it or not, worked as a mortuary assistant for some years in Florida and he did the diagnosis. It may simply be a bad cold, though I admit it doesn't feel like that right now. I cough and I am running a fever. Gus has been extremely attentive, so you have no worries. As soon as conditions improve, Cindy has promised to fly in and whisk me away to Anchorage.

I promise I will tell you if I don't improve rapidly. Promise me that you won't worry overmuch.

The last three-quarters of the trip—from the point, really, where I sent my last batch of letters—was no picnic. Even Martha, who is unflappable and as unyielding to her body as any human I have ever met, had difficulty. We got hit by two whiteouts, where the snow came so thick and so fast that dogs swirled around you and then disappeared, only to reemerge from a different angle. Every sight and sound seemed reinvented a moment after you saw or heard it. I can't describe it adequately. It is nearly worse than having no sight—it is a shredded vision, and it lends a nightmarish quality to even the smallest movements.

I have to sleep. My hands still feel frozen. They have thawed, I'm sure, but they don't feel as if they have. I am taking aspirin and drinking plenty of fluids. Starve a fever, feed a cold? Or is it the other way around? I can never remember.

I'll write again later. I know you are impatient to hear about Paul...

Sam

Hadley—

I am still sorting my emotions about the trip. And what I saw. And what I felt. It was more than you can imagine, and less in some way, too.

The trip: We ran into three hunters out on snowmobiles. They call them simply "sleds" or "machines" but never snowmobiles. Native Americans. Inuit. I'm not sure what the proper name is, but Martha knew them, and they had the appearance of Native Americans. You have never met three more taciturn men in all your days. They each wore a blue parka, each wore fur-lined pants, and each wore the most massive pair of boots imaginable. They never took off their goggles, so something both modern and otherworldly lingered about them. They carried large rifles in holsters attached to their sleds. These were cowboys—or Indians, I suppose—on twenty-first-century horses, riding the last plains. They stopped when they saw us. One had a thermos full of coffee and brandy and he gave us a small sip. Very strong and sugary, and delicious. They liked Martha, she said later, because she ran dogs. They see machines as inevitable, and necessary, but machines break down and cost money, while dogs, she said, fill the heart.

They had a butchered caribou attached to the back sled, pulled behind on an empty toboggan-type rig. The caribou had been quartered and was frozen rigid. They had kept the head, the antlers strapped under a bungee, and you know how these things appear: bright black eyes dulled with frost. They thought it peculiar that I wanted to examine the carcass, but how many times, I asked them, does someone from the lower forty-eight get to see a caribou? Anyway, the dogs pulled to get closer to it, and it became a bit of a mess with the dogs straining and reacting to the smell of the body, and the men finding the whole thing amusing.

Martha told me to give my letters to the smallest of the three. His name was Abe. I had already addressed the letters on the possibility of running into someone. I gave him twenty dollars for postage and a tip. Abe had a hard time understanding why a man in the middle of a dogsled journey needed to mail a letter. I told him it was an electric bill, but he didn't think it was funny. He took the letters and stuffed them in his pocket.

We talked for a while about the weather. They predicted a change, more snow, dropping temperature. That concurred with the last report Martha had from her sources. Then we spent a while showing them Martha's GPS. They liked that technology and asked how much it cost. Our exchange struck me as two boats encountering each other on the sea, but we inhabited a solid ocean, a landscape of whiteness and wind and humpy veins of earth and grass. That's all. The conversation proved notable by its utility. We traded information, even mail, then cast off.

They pulled away in three putrid puffs of gasoline. I was

glad to be back with the dogs, but I couldn't help again asking Martha if I could have taken a snowmobile to Paul's wreckage.

"No," she said, "we couldn't get there on a sled."

"Why not?"

"We have to bushwhack and we have to go across water. You can't bushwhack with a sled. You'd have to hike three or four miles in difficult country. Don't worry. You're using the right approach."

I felt better knowing that I hadn't turned a day's outing into a ten-day dogsled trip just for aesthetic reasons. So we mushed on. We did not cross another snowmobile trail for the rest of the trip, nor did we see another human.

Soup break. I promise I will get to the whole thing after a nap. I'm sorry, I am still feeling a little tired. Gus insists I eat to keep up my strength. He's an old broody hen.

* *

Okay, back. Full of vim and vigor. What is vim, anyway? All right, I won't get sidetracked. My mind is chasing rabbits a little, though. Medicine and fatigue, I guess.

So, after the three hunters left, Martha and I began the final push into the crash site. We tacked north. What had been a sort of snowmobile trail in places now gave way to full bush. We slowed and picked our way along. It didn't take long for me to understand why we had to approach on dogsled. Any number of times we bogged down into drifts, or

113

had to circle slowly around blowdowns, and the dogs showed their tenacity and strength. More than once they went right into my heart—a little corny, but true. On one occasion we came to a small mound covered by saplings and thornbushes. It didn't look like much until we realized the snow had drifted against it, pushing up to nearly ten feet high. The dogs couldn't get a purchase; it wasn't frozen and it wasn't soft enough for them to chest through. Martha yelled "On-by" as loud as she could and the dogs heaved and pushed and waded. At times they actually went under the snow. Imagine it—ten dogs burrowing and pulling and nothing of them visible except now and then a tip of the tail. They might have carried the sled down into the earth, for all anyone would know, but they yanked and pulled, and banged the sled against the saplings, and Martha shoved the sled handles this way and that, still yelling, and then little by little the dogs emerged. Magnificent, I promise you, sweetheart. At one point the sled tipped nearly vertical, and Martha almost fell back with it, but instead she grabbed the crossbar and yelled "Get up" and the dogs put their shoulders into it and dragged the sled up and over. They did it for her. It seemed to me that this was a fulfillment of a pact between them—that she would do anything for them, and they for her.

We camped that evening (or afternoon…there is little daylight left) one day's journey from Paul's site. It was the last clear night we had, and the northern lights came out and began dancing as you can only see them in picture books or a nature program. I don't know what to think of the northern lights. I watched them for a long time, checking them as we set up tents, fed the dogs, and so on. I understand the phenomenon a little, and know it comes from magnetic waves, but I can never make myself believe such a thing exists. Nothing so dramatic, so vivid, can result from the collision of atoms or ions or whatever it is that waves and glows. But it does, of course. Green bands, and curtains of phosphorescent gold. Everything moving. A door to heaven, really, and right beyond it the thing we seek, whatever it is.

I want you to know this, darling. I wandered off for a few minutes by myself. I don't know why, but I knelt down and watched the northern lights pulse and dance and I sent my soul to Paul. I don't believe in God. I can't. But I believed in our son. I told him that I was here, that I loved him, that his mother could barely go on without him, that if I pushed him too hard to come on this adventure that I was sorry. So sorry. That I would give anything—limb, life—to have him back. I told him that he had been the best of both of us, that if such a thing proved possible in the afterlife, we would not rest until we reunited with him. I said that his parents loved him. I said his leaving had broken our hearts. And then I said goodbye to him.

I don't know what any of this means, or if it means anything at all. I teeter between finding it enormously important one moment and insignificant the next. But for what it's worth, Hadley, I felt connected to our son in that instant.

No great miraculous change in my heart, or new under-standing resulted, I'm afraid. I merely felt that I had put something in order, arranged it properly, and that perhaps was sufficient.

Later that night, snow began to fall. It had been falling off and on for a while, brief flurries, but suddenly the world be-came still and you could hear the slightest movement from the dogs. Then the hiss of the stove became louder, and the tent ceased flapping, and it began to storm. At first it felt welcome. I hadn't been conscious of how intently I had been listening to the wind. But then the snow increased, and Martha sat up and looked around, and her restlessness affected me.

"We'll be digging out tomorrow morning," she said.

"How much?"

"Hard to know."

"Will it prevent us from getting there?"

"No," she said. "We'll get there but we won't stay long, if that's okay. We should head back unless we want to bivouac for a week or so."

"Okay, we'll make it quick," I said.

"I don't want to rush you. We're not in danger. We are just going to be slowed considerably."

"I understand."

"The danger is always in between. Pushing when you shouldn't push. Staying when you shouldn't stay."

The next morning we woke to more snow. Snow covered

the tent. The dogs had made a small warren of deep burrows where they had slept. They shook their coats free as we gave them a morning meal. Martha performed everything evenly, but without her usual enthusiasm. What had been a short, cumbersome trip had transformed into a more risky proposition. I nearly said we could turn back, that I had what I wanted, but that would have been insane. For better or worse, I could not come so close and then leave without seeing the site.

It was hard going, as the adventure books always describe these things. We lost all semblance of trail. I followed Martha. She waded behind the sled and kept one hand tied by a short length of rope to the handlebar. We didn't run so much as slog. It was exhausting—for us, for the dogs, for everything. The snow did not relent, but came in pants of intensity, occasionally bursting so hard from behind the mountains that we had to stop and wait for it to allow us to proceed. We crossed a dozen swampy gunnels of mud and muck and snow, each one bordered by hummocks of knotty grass. Moose country. Puckerbrush.

I also began to cough on this day. A cold, I figured. But it burned in my veins and several times Martha asked if I was all right. I didn't feel all right exactly, but there was little point in complaining. In late morning Martha jammed her snow hook into the ground and walked back to me. Nothing unusual in that, except this time she held out her GPS and said, "We're here, Sam."

I looked at it. The coordinates matched what we knew from police records. This place, this acre, this was where he died.

What can I tell you that will soothe your heart, Hadley? It was not a pretty place, nor a horrible place. Moose country, as I said. In summer, a bog. Few trees of any size, although a boreal forest seemed to begin a few miles to the east. A valley, really, but a valley on an Alaskan scale. I am not sure what I expected to see. Had any trace remained of the deaths associated with the accident—which was unlikely in the extreme—snow had already covered it. The land did not appear gouged or disfigured by the plane. The heat of whatever had happened has long since cooled.

The plane exists, Hadley. I saw it. Snow had covered most of it, and the nose had broken away. The wings had sheared off, but the mute aluminum tube still resembled an airplane. A strut of the right wing remained intact. A red stripe—I don't know why, but it transfixed me—ran down the top of the fuselage. I walked to the plane and placed my hand on it. Then I turned away.

Martha busied herself turning the sleds. The snow intensified. I did not cry, Hadley. I'm not sure what I felt. Loss, and sadness and love. I left the picture of our family beside the plane. I kissed it, said goodbye again to Paul, and put the picture under a few handfuls of snow. He is not there, sweetheart. He is gone. You knew that already, but I didn't somehow. I am glad I saw the spot, but it is just a windy knob in a bog no one will visit again for many decades. I felt Paul more clearly, more resolutely, the previous night when the northern lights flickered and danced and snow hung just beyond the horizon. Oh, my son.

You asked if he felt pain or terror, and I can't speak authoritatively to that. I have wondered it myself. I received few clues from the wreckage, except that the nose of the plane had disappeared, which meant the impact had been significant. Draw from that what you will. I'm so sorry you have to consider these possibilities. When I am feeling strong and positive about Paul, I imagine him using his skills and intelligence to think of ways to survive. I cannot picture him abandoning hope, so no, I do not think he felt abject terror on the descent. The plane did not fall nose first, not vertically—it came in on an angle, as if they might be able to crash-land. From that detail I believe Paul retained hopes of surviving the crash. He would not have despaired or given up prematurely. That was not his character. He would have braced himself, knowing it was hellishly dangerous, but he was young and strong and would have seen himself making it through. That's what I believe. From the appearance of the nose section—from where it had been, rather, and please don't feel you need to read this if you don't want to—the impact was massive and overwhelming. He died quickly, darling. He died all at once.

I said something for the pilot, Kilkenny. I had blocked his name so many times, that I wondered at how easily it came to mind beside the plane. For what it was worth, I said I forgave him. I don't know if I meant it or not, or even if I had a right to forgive anyone, but he died here, too, and I no longer wanted to hold him responsible. Ice. Flight. They perished together, Paul and Kilkenny, and I hope they drew some solace from their companionship.

You wait, of course, for some sign in these moments, but I saw nothing. Too much snow fell from above. We didn't stay long. When Martha had the dogs turned, ready to head back, she came to me and asked if I was all right. Did I want to stay longer? Did I want to camp there for the night? She hugged me briefly, said she was sorry for our loss, then saw that I was determined to follow her back. She took her sled back the way we had come.

I couldn't speak and I couldn't move with any purpose. I felt myself floating—maybe my illness, but also the sense of loss overwhelming me. I went to the front of my team and knelt between Grabby and Sneak and put my face on their fur. They were impatient to go and kept darting their heads past me, watching Martha's team advance. Maybe this time they were saying "On-by" to me. The dead must find their own way, if there is a way, and the living have no choice but to go on living. On-by.

I looked one last time at the fuselage, then lifted the snow hook from where Martha had wedged it, yelled "Huphuphup" and left. The dogs pulled like maniacs to catch Martha's team. In minutes snow obscured any last glimpse of the plane.

So that was my great quest, sweetheart. A fool's errand or not, I don't know. We had a difficult time on the return. We had to wait out one storm for more than a day. Cold and miserable. Martha told me stories of polar exploration, which I enjoyed. She is writing a book and so the tales were fresh in her mind. I told her about covering sports and some of my own adventures.

Our last night in the tent the temperature dropped to well below zero—probably 30 below. I have never felt cold to equal it. The dogs went under the snow immediately when we halted, and they refused to come out for food. A few trees exploded—the sap became so cold that the wood contracted and snapped. Then on the lake to our west the ice began booming and moving and it gave a haunted feeling to the night. It is a hard country, but I could see how one could grow to love it. Martha and I did not stay up long. We went to sleep, eager to have morning arrive. In the middle of the night Grabby slithered into my sleeping bag. You would not have thought it possible, but she nosed her way in and before I could prevent it she had burrowed down beside me. Her fur brushing against me was cold, but eventually she warmed me, and I learned at last the true meaning of a one- (or two-) dog night.

Everything had lost the capacity to yield by the next

morning—the dogs' lines curled like tired inner tubes, and the sled runners clung to the ice beneath them. This form of traveling is mental more than anything else. You must be optimistic and solid, or the cold will draw you into it and exert its power. Martha seemed to sense our languor, because she repeated often that we would make it home that day. That was the carrot. By this time, I'll admit, my cough had grown quite ragged. I coughed most of the night and all morning on the sled. Martha turned around on her sled frequently to check me, and I knew she weighed pushing harder to get us home, or taking it easier to accommodate my condition.

We arrived at two o'clock. Swahili met us and took over the dogs. She hugged Martha and she hugged me. Then, like that, it was over.

Sam

Hadley—

I hope I haven't been a complete cad not to have asked about your wrist. I hope it's feeling better now and mending properly. Is there anything more slippery than cold rocks by the ocean? But I know how you love getting to places like that, and the return the sea gives to you, so it would be futile for me to tell you to avoid them or take a friend. I'm sorry I didn't ask sooner in these pages. I have been preoccupied with the trip to the plane and my own feelings and I neglected you on that count. Forgive me. You know, of course, I only want good things for you.

I am thinking about you all the time. All the time. Do you know that inner voice we have, our conscience, our personal PA system, whatever the heck it is? Mine has your voice. That might make me borderline schizophrenic, but there it is. Sometimes I don't know if I am listening to my voice or yours. Maybe love is a confusion of voices.

And I want a hundred answers from you. Will you keep the house? What have you decided? How are your paintings coming? I love the sketches you included. You have a gift, as I've always known. And did Julie arrive? How is she? I have a wonderful image of you two warm beside the fire and the wind giving you a pleasant pane rattling. Your Irish blood responds to all that banshee moaning. But it is working toward Christmas and I like thinking of you two together, the white lights of dim restaurants, the smell of pine and peppermint. Tell Julie as much about my findings here as you feel you should. She is a lovely young woman and I miss her in our lives.

I had a rocky couple of nights—bad cough, high temperature—but I am feeling better now. Gus came close to calling for an emergency evacuation. Snow still had us locked in, so it would have been quite a big deal to have summoned the EMTs. But they would have come if called, putting their own lives at risk. I suspect I came with the germ of the pneumonia in me. It wasn't all the dogs and the snow. I will be better soon, so no worries.

I have to inform you about one more thing, then I'll wrap this up. Apparently the charter airline company that carried Paul northward is holding some of his possessions. His effects, they called it. Kilkenny's wife wants to see me. She said if I am passing back through Anchorage—and of course I am—she hoped I would stop by to see her. I am not sure why, but I have misgivings about seeing her. It feels like a little mystery. Why didn't she simply say what she wanted with me? Anyway, I will stop and see her on my way out. I hope to be back in Seattle by Christmas Day.

Back to you, Hadley. Always back to you.

Sam

December 12

Dear Sam,

I don't know what to say, where to begin. You saw the plane, you stood there in the spot where he fell to earth. Your difficulties getting there . . . to what really is and was the end of the world to me. I'm sorry you've had such a hard time. Sam, I'm glad you were there—that you laid eyes on the plane, and that you touched it, and that you kissed the picture and left it there. You did that for both of us. Thank you.

You're lucky to be alive, aren't you? That's what I get from this batch of letters. Thank goodness for your intrepid mail system. You were right all along, and I really needed to read these as soon as possible after you wrote them. You're sick, and I'm worried. Pneumonia, really? Sam . . .

* *

It's sinking in, that you actually made it to the site, saw where Paul died, that you were right there where he was. It always sounded so distant and remote, and obviously it was. But now that I know you did it, that you went through so much planning and traveling and hardship to get there, I wish I'd gone, too. So much danger. So much lost.

I'd expected to cry when I read your letters, but I couldn't. I just read straight through, wanting to find out what happened, what you saw, and whether you're okay. I had all the information, but I couldn't feel it ... maybe I couldn't let myself. Wide awake, here in my little rented house, it would have been too much, too deep—or maybe it's just that I'm too alone here to let the feelings come. So I had to wait for sleep to take over.

But it didn't. I just lay awake, and I swear I could hear your dogs barking ... Jenny and Penny ... I love that you have dog sisters. Family sticking together—that's what always mattered to us. I thought I heard the sisters starting to howl and cry. My eyes were closed, and I imagined I was with you right there, in the spot where you found Paul's plane. I was with you and the dogs ... and we were with Paul.

The mound ... that word stung me when I read it on the page, a few pages before you write about finding the plane. "Mound" sounds like what it is—funereal. I guess I fell asleep ... because I swear I saw the mound; it was part of the landscape—endless and stark and white. It was covered with snow, just like you said, and I saw the saplings. I reached out, to pull myself up, and I grasped one of the thornbushes you wrote about, and it pricked my thumb ... blood on the snow.

And it melted ... rivulets of white and blue water, mingled with my blood as it flowed harder from my thumb. And then it wasn't—my skin was healed, and I was digging, in such a panic—my heart frozen and caught in my throat, clawing through the snow to the frozen ground.

I'm telling you the truth—this really happened. People lose their minds with grief. Having our son die . . . how can I even explain this? Or do I have to explain at all? My mind takes flights, Sam. It's how I can go to him. Go to you, too. I'm not sure whether I was awake when I saw all this, or whether I was fast asleep.

You'd said the plane was there, but in my dream it was gone. All I found was the picture you'd left. And it was ruined. The snow and melting ice and my blood had blurred the image, made the paper so delicate it fell apart when I touched it. And that's when I started to cry. My heart just broke open, and I stood there holding the soggy pieces of paper, trying to put them back together, just wanting to see your faces—our faces. You and me and Paul . . .

I started to howl, just like the dogs—Jenny and Penny were with me, right by my side. I could feel their wet fur through my jeans. They were pressing against me, holding me up. And then I heard Paul say, "Mom?"

I turned around, and he was there with you. And this is so strange—but you were both the same age. He was twenty, just the age he was when he died, and so were you—my young husband, your hair and beard still brown—and you both were smiling. I looked at you and wondered how I hadn't known your trip to Alaska had been to save Paul— how had I thought he was dead?

And I reached out to hold you both, and the dogs began to bark again, and that's when I woke up.

This is the part you won't believe: when I opened my eyes, I saw the most ghostly green light at the window. I thought maybe the people next door had put up Christmas lights. But I got out of bed and crossed the room, and it was the northern lights.

The first time I've ever seen them. I'd always thought we would see them together. When I think of the celestial shows we've seen—the Perseid and Lyrid meteor showers, the Southern Cross, total eclipses of the sun and moon, Hale-Bopp, nights of Venus, mornings of Mars...why did we always have our eyes trained on the sky? But we did, we always did, and we never saw the northern lights together.

I stood at the window, touching the cold glass so I would feel it under my fingertips and know I was really awake, and I stared out at the green and gold—just the way you described it in your letter. And you know, Sam—I know you sent it to me. I know that you sent the northern lights from Alaska to Maine so I would know you were with me.

And I want to tell you right now, more than anything I want you to know that I am with you, too. I swear I am, Sam.

I wish I could send the northern lights back your way so

you would know. I'm thinking so hard right now, directing my thoughts up there. Here's what I want to say:

We loved him, and we loved each other. We were a family, and we still are. Not even his death can take him away from us or us from him. I feel him with me, Sam. And you, too. Close your eyes and know I'm holding your hand, thanking you for what you did, for going to Paul, for bringing our son back to me.

* *

I can't sleep. I tried, but it's not going to happen.

Do you know Rumi's poem "Love Dogs"? I've been thinking about it, ever since reading your last batch of letters. It's beautiful and haunting, and makes me think of you. It speaks of a dog moaning, and his master hearing. That ineffable connection between two souls.

> *The grief you cry out from*
> *draws you toward union.*

Can you see why that line makes me think of you, especially now? The poem is for you, but also for Grabby, Sneak,

Wiley, Dash, Blondie, Dutch, Snowball, Kya, and, especially, my girls—Jenny and Penny.

And for Martha. Thank her for me . . . or maybe I'll thank her myself.

Hadley

To Martha Rich:

December 12

Dear Martha,

I just sent Sam a letter asking him to thank you for me, but I decided that what I really want to do is write you myself. I need to thank you for...well, for more things than you can know. Starting with helping Sam visit the site of our son's death. I'm not sure how much he's told you about us, about the history between us, and how I felt about his trip to the Arctic, to visit Paul's crash site.

I didn't want him to go at all. It wasn't long after we got the news of Paul's death that Sam began to think about going to Alaska. Not to bring home Paul's body—the Alaskan authorities made those arrangements, and we buried him near our home—but to see the spot, to lay eyes on it, to touch the ground. I think part of him believed it wasn't really true, that until he actually *went* there, saw it, he could believe that it was all a terrible mistake. Maybe that's why it took him so long to go. He could never bear to visit Paul's grave. But he was determined, finally, to see where he died.

At first it was assumed that I would go with him. To Sam, it was our duty as Paul's parents. Now, reading his letters, I have to ask myself many questions...why didn't I want to go? Was it really because I felt I'd had more than I could take? Seeing our son's remains, seeing his name on his head-stone? Paul's body was home—he was already buried, so why would I want to travel into the terrible territory that had taken his life?

Sam became—there's only one word for it—obsessed. He lived, slept, and ate Alaska. He took many assignments during this time, and he'd come home from wherever he was with stories of people he'd met, people who'd gone into the bush. He researched the ways to reach Paul's crash site, learned that there were only two ways—helicopter and dog-sled. Then he learned that the only helicopter pilot stationed up past Laika Star, a guy who'd been taking trappers and fisherman into the country, had died in a crash. So then it came down to dogs and hiking.

This is all stuff that you know. Sam likes to talk—I'm sure you know that by now, too, sharing a tent with him. I loved that about him, from the time we were young. The way he would tell a story, going on and around, weaving it all together. Other women complain their husbands don't talk; that was never the case with Sam. So I'm wondering what, how much, he told you . . . I wonder how he presented it to you. I find myself, a little, wanting to defend myself to you.

It doesn't matter, though . . . the important thing is that you helped him get there safely, helped him leave the photo at the site. That was his idea, but in the end it meant so much to me. I can only imagine how it was for Sam, to do that. I know he got sick on that last leg, and he's never been good at taking care of himself. He's a force of nature, and nothing can keep him down. I hope he's doing what the doctor tells him.

Maybe we'll meet someday, Martha. Until then, please know you have my deepest thanks and respect. May your holidays be bright...

Yours,
Hadley West

Dear Sam,

It's getting close to Christmas, and I miss you terribly. Julie is coming out tomorrow, and she'll stay the night. I'm looking forward to seeing her, and I wasn't last week; I think it's a combination of getting your letters, knowing that things are at rest in a new way—that you've been there, borne witness, left our picture there, and you're almost on the way home. That plus Julie herself. You're right—we always enjoyed her. She's a good girl, and I love her for wanting to stay in our lives.

Sam, by now I assume Martha has told you I wrote to her. Just a thank-you note to let her know how much I appreciate what she did for you. Your letters are full of so many names, people I feel I know—or should know. Gus, Cindy, even poor Kilkenny. You mentioned that you said something for him. You didn't say "prayer" because that's not your way. It's not really mine either, but I stopped into the island chapel this morning and lit candles. One for you, one for Paul, and one for Kilkenny.

And now I'm back home, sitting by the kitchen window, looking out into the darkness. Some of the houses are strung with white lights; I can see them in the distance. The house next door has Christmas candles in the windows, and I can see their tree all lit up in the living room.

December hit the island full-force—not so much with snow and ice, although there's plenty of both—but with a hollow wind that never lets up. If loneliness was a weather pattern, this would be it. It's easy to have the feeling that you're all alone in the world, that the wind could blow you off the land straight into the sea. So there's something like whistling in the dark here, the way the islanders light candles and brighten their houses with strings of light. It's touching, S.

Where are you tonight? What are you doing, who are you with? Are there candles burning, are you by the fireside? Are you getting close to civilization? Will this be the last letter I send via our Arctic/Monhegan Special Delivery? You mentioned stopping by the charter company, and going to see Kilkenny's wife. I suppose I've blocked both of those things out. I wonder what she'll say to you, give you, things having to do with Paul. Maybe all these white lights glowing through the trees are helping me whistle in the dark, too. It's not so scary knowing I'm not alone.

Your voice. You asked me about the inner voice. The one I hear at night, when the lights are out, when Cat is asleep at the foot of the bed, and the wind is howling up the headlands and into the pines, that's yours. It always has been. And even with all our changes and separation—or maybe because of them—it's still yours.

Confusion abounds, S. My neighbors are gathered around the hearth, getting ready for Christmas. The lobster season

began on December 1, and in spite of the terrible weather, the boats go out every morning. I try to imagine what it must be like for Turner and the others, motoring out into the ocean before dawn, coming home after dark. They must see all the lights and feel warmer just knowing their families are waiting for them.

Your letters have been that for me. I wait for delivery every day, every morning, wondering whether there'll be something from you. Today I got papers from the lawyer—he had a real estate person appraise the house and orchard, and he wanted me to sign them and return them right away. The rumors have started, and people are interested. Someone wants to bulldoze the orchard and build houses.

I tore the papers up. I don't know about anything but this: I'm not selling. No one's building houses in the orchard. That much I know for sure. That orchard is ours. Ida Reds, Macouns, and Winesaps. The best apples anywhere.

Something else came in today's mail: a court date. We're what's called "on the docket." Our lawyers are scheduled to show up at Superior Court on January 16, stand before a judge, and complete our divorce. Neither of us is required to be present at the dissolution of our marriage.

You know that question I mentioned to you a while back? I asked myself what I want. I've spent a good spell out here asking and asking.

All I know is, I want us to keep writing to each other.

Hadley

Dear Sam,

Julie just left . . . I walked her to the dock and saw her off on the mail boat. She stood in the stern waving until the boat disappeared around the edge of Manana, heading toward the mainland. We had such a wonderful time together, but do you know—I think it's the last time she's going to come.

For the first time, I questioned her more deeply about Paul and why he left when he did—why he couldn't wait till graduation. And what she told me—I'm not over it yet. Get ready, Sam . . .

She got pregnant. They found out during Easter break, the year before he left. She said that her first reaction was excitement—and so was Paul's. They loved each other, and they felt the way—I guess the way we did. But then the struggle began. The torment—that was the word she used. They were so young, and in school, and she couldn't imagine having a baby and continuing at Amherst.

She weighed leaving college for a year, having the baby. She told me Paul wanted to marry her—to him, it wasn't even a question. He wanted to tell us—he told her he knew we would help them out with rent and expenses, all of it. She told me to remember back then, that Easter . . . how she had come to visit us, and how I'd made her a basket filled with colored eggs and chocolates, just like Paul's. And she was sick the whole time—she was so pale and sick to her stomach, and I held her hair while she threw up in the upstairs bathroom in the middle of the night.

And I *did* remember, Sam. You were in bed, but getting ready to leave in the morning for a trip, I forget where now. And Paul was pacing the hallway, up and down, while I tended to Julie. I remember telling him to go to bed, settle down—she had a stomach flu and would be fine. But he wouldn't—he stayed right outside the bathroom door.

I remember helping Julie back into bed, getting her a cold cloth for her head, asking her if she felt like a glass of ginger ale. She just shook her head, buried her face in the pillow. I remember wondering if she'd had too much to drink— they'd gone out with some of their friends, and I thought maybe she'd overdone it. It didn't occur to me that she was pregnant—why not? I wonder now. It didn't even cross my mind, at least not consciously.

But she was, eight weeks, and they were going to tell us that weekend. And then—what she had wasn't morning sickness, but a miscarriage. That night, after I tucked her in, Paul sneaked into her room, and she told him she was having cramps. He stayed with her, held her hand. She said he ran down around dawn, to get us to help her, but we'd left— I had to drive you to the airport, and then stop at Gillian's house on the way back.

As I spun back, trying to put together my memory of

the weekend, it's all hazy—I do remember driving you, and I think I remember picking Gillian up and going to the museum for lunch, and I vaguely recall coming home and finding a note from Paul—that Julie had decided to go home early, and he was driving her. If anything, I was probably happy at the prospect of a day or so alone with him—such a rare thing at that time of all our lives.

But what I'm sure about is how quiet he was when he got back. He'd spent the night at her house, driven back home the next day. And you know, Sam—he never really seemed all himself after that. Remember how we worried about him that spring, how he just seemed to disappear into himself when he came home the next time, and for the summer? And then he told us he wanted to take time off . . . that he'd found the village in Alaska where he wanted to go and live and teach . . .

Julie told me it wasn't because he'd stopped loving her, or because he'd stopped wanting to finish Amherst—it was because he'd realized that he loved everything too much. He'd fallen in love with their baby even before it was born, before it had a chance to be born. She told me she'd started bleeding heavily in the car right after they left the house, and he'd been so worried, he'd driven her straight to the nearest hospital. She'd gone straight into the ER, and it turned out she was miscarrying.

She'd made him promise not to tell us—and she didn't tell her parents, either. She felt ashamed, confused, all of it.

And since there was no baby, why muddy—as she put it—everyone's view of her? I tried telling her we would have loved her anyway, it wouldn't have changed our feelings at all; she said she knows that now, but back then she felt ashamed. Paul understood her wish, and of course he'd done as she asked. But meanwhile she could see it had changed him—he went through a depression that spring, realizing how delicate life could be, and how powerful love was, and not knowing how to reconcile any of it. She said that when they were honest with each other, they were partly relieved by what had happened—losing the baby. And that troubled Paul.

He had to leave because of love, that's what she told me. Because it was both too much and not enough. He'd always loved nature so much, and the idea of going to extremes, to the very top of the world, to help poor people—give them some of what he had, what he knew, what he'd learned—while, he thought, finding a way to learn how to survive in harsh conditions, to enjoy the simple joys of life while struggling to endure hard things, he thought that might be the best way to figure out how to go on.

That's what she said he said—"go on." I told her it made him sound almost suicidal, as if he were having doubts about this life. And she said no, it was the opposite. He was wildly alive. She hadn't wanted him to go, but she'd known she couldn't stop him. Besides, the miscarriage had woken her up, made her question a lot of the status quo and what she'd always imagined she wanted. She knew that she wanted Paul, and they both wanted children someday, but she also realized she had to make a mark on the world in her own way. And she wanted and needed time alone, to think about what that would be.

She said she and Paul stayed in constant touch, all through his journey from home to Alaska, right up until the day he flew to Anchorage. They talked and texted and emailed; he'd warned her that contact would be difficult once he got to the village, but that he'd be with her all the time—all she had to do was think of him, and he'd feel it, and he'd be thinking of her, too. She said that she felt him "out there," is the way she put it, for two years after he died. And then . . . not so much. The feeling of him faded. She'd search for him in her mind, but she couldn't find him anymore.

She told me all this now for two reasons. One, because you're in Alaska, you've done it—gone to find his plane. Somehow that seems to comfort her, as I've realized it does me as well. She's sad that we've broken up and asked me more than once if I was sure it was the right thing. She sounded so mature, as if we were the troubled kids, you and I, throwing something precious away. Then she said the funniest thing: she said, "Sam and Hadley—you two always seemed so perfect together. Just the way Paul and I would have wanted to be."

Here's the other thing. It's hard to write, Sam. Julie's with someone new now. He's not Paul, she said—he never could be. He's very different, big and athletic—played football for Michigan. Born and raised in Chicago. But he's an environmentalist, an activist—he's a lawyer, went to Georgetown, and she loves and admires him. His name is Matt Brady. They started seeing each other last June, and they've started talking about getting married. She said he supports her decision to go to law school—she's taking the LSATs soon. And they're thinking about a summer wedding . . .

She took two days off from work to come here—she's been working in New York for an environmental advocacy firm. They take action, which is to say bring lawsuits to bring about change. She's passionate about her work, just the way she used to be about everything else—college, mountain climbing, Paul. From the minute she arrived, we started talking, and basically never stopped.

She worked to keep oil companies from drilling in the Chukchi Sea and Arctic National Wildlife Refuge. She showed me amazing photographs by Subhankar Banerjee— he went up there and took the surreal, poetic pictures of the region—my favorite is of a herd of caribou migrating over the sea ice—taken from the sky, they look like ants on a blue-green ribbon, just moving across the land in grace and profusion. I saw the picture and immediately flashed on your letter, the dead caribou you saw being carted by the three hunters on "sleds." You would love the picture . . .

143

these caribou are so alive and on the move. Julie left the book for me—an exhibition catalogue called *The Last Wilderness*—and I'll save it for you.

Her current project has to do with restricting the Navy's use of low-frequency sonar across 70 percent of the world's oceans. What I didn't know is that the sonar emits dangerously high decibel levels that harm marine mammals. It's one of the reasons for mass strandings and death of whales and dolphins. She reminded me of how intelligent they are, and of the pain they feel from the sonar. It causes staggeringly sharp pain and acute disorientation.

We settled in while the snow fell, and I remembered instantly why we liked her so much right away . . . and why Paul loved her. She's so intelligent and kind, and she's lovely—that porcelain skin, and long dark hair, and those gray-green eyes. Hearing her talk about the environment, hearing her fervor—of course I thought of Paul, and of how alike they were. He was every bit as mad about the things that drove him as she is about her work.

As important as the projects she's working on, she realized she could make a bigger difference if she could actually work on the briefs, go to court. She said that with the environment in such fragile shape, she feels pressure to contribute her time and work right now, at the highest level she possibly can. I listened to her with such pride and admiration—for her, but also for Paul, that he recognized so young a girl who was truly his—excuse the phrase—soul mate. I really feel that they were that for each other. They wanted to change the world together.

And now she's going to do that with someone else.

Sam . . . I'm both so happy for her and so brokenhearted. To look into her beautiful eyes and think of the baby she and Paul would have had. Almost did have . . . I can't believe he went through all that, and how it informed his decision to leave school and go to Alaska, without telling us. I held her hand, and thought of Paul holding her hand, and we both started to cry. I pulled out your letters, let her read the one about you finding the plane, leaving the picture.

"He would have liked that," she said. "He would have liked that so much . . ."

She asked me to give you her love. And she left, and said she'd be back next year—she'd come to the house. I told her to bring her guy, that we'd love to meet him, and she said she would—but I know she won't.

Oh, Sam. And you know, I wouldn't want her to. I really wouldn't. Does that make me terrible?

We almost had a grandchild. I don't know why, but right now I'm holding on to that thought very tightly. Paul would have married her, and he would have been such a good father. Because he learned from the best.

Can this be over? The grief, and where it's led us? Sam, I'm not sure I can stand Christmas without you.

H.

ORION

✳ ✳ ✳

I knew the stars, the flowers, and the birds,

The grey and wintry sides of many glens,

And did but half remember human words.

> —*John Millington Synge*
> from "Prelude"

December 18

Hadley—

Your letters arrived almost as I started out the door of Laika Star. I stayed there much longer than I had anticipated, but it was good. How strange and fateful our timing is and always has been. I am writing this on the small plane that is taking me to Anchorage. Gus's girlfriend, Cindy, is flying me. I should be looking out the window and appreciating the view—a great white sheet, like furniture stored for winter—but I am tired of Alaska. Cindy understood without asking. One can sink into this land and risk never coming out. I need to leave soon or something will be broken inside me. I'm not sure how to explain it, but I know it in my clearest mind.

I read your letters and hardly know how to respond. I need to think a little more about it, about all that you included. I also hope that you will not think it peculiar if we continue to write letters. I will be able to pick up a phone and call you within the hour, but I am reminded that we have been kinder and more open to one another in these letters than we have been in person or on the phone—for too long. I suspect we are making a record, or a map, in these

149

letters that a phone call would undermine. Perhaps it forces us to slow down and examine what we want and what we say. I thought the other day that whatever happens finally between us, these letters represent the best of us. It is too easy to talk things away. I want to talk with you in a slower world.

I'm thinking of you, Hadley. I'm hoping your wrist is better and that Christmas is bringing all its sweetness to you. I remember how you love this season, and how you kept Christmas well, as Dickens said of Scrooge, and how your painter's sensibility wrings all the beauty out of the light and fragrance and makes it a gift to those around you. It sounds so strange and oddly 1950s to say it, but I loved how you kept house, Hadley. I don't know if I ever said that quite so plainly before. I loved the home you made for us, the appeal to our senses, the beauty and arrangements, the still lifes you created and thought no one noticed. Paul and I would find them and marvel—a bowl of apples beside a piece of barbed wire, a length of barn board beside a metal last—but we depended on them and could not imagine living without them. I long for that. I can close my eyes and it doesn't matter where you are—I know you have a fire going, and you will find large, knotty logs, and you will have found bittersweet and winterberry and braided them into whisks, and you will have something good on the stove, mulled wine, or black cider, and it is not a pose, it is simply an extension of you and how you interact with the world. To be with you is to be swept into that delightful corner. You know what I mean. Beauty is truth and all that. You live that ideal more closely than anyone I have ever met.

I confess I feel slightly overwhelmed with all you have imparted. Julie, a miscarriage. I have difficulty getting my mind around it. And I'll admit, too, that my health is still not 100 percent. Gus nursed me along and Cindy has been wonderful—she is a tall redhead with freckles and enormous breasts, a kind of Alaskan cowgirl by way of Tulsa, and she has a tattoo of a rose across the side of her throat—but I am weak a portion of the time. I'm getting better, but if it takes me a while to digest what you've written, please understand.

In fact, I have to stop here. We are following the Yukon River south. Our shadow flies beside us along the ground, going east and south toward you.

Sam

H—

It is evening and I am safely ensconed, if that's the right term for it, in a Fairtown Motel in downtown Anchorage. I thought about trying to follow your dictum that by discovering new lodgings—B&B's, rented rooms, the little byways—we discover where we are, but then rejected it in favor of plain old-fashioned American vanilla comfort. See, I am a peasant at heart! Besides, I wanted a big, comfortable bed, a TV with a laser-accurate remote. I tell myself, as I tell you, that it is part of my job to catch up on sports, but mostly I like the abundant light right now, the solid warmth, the sense that I am anonymous. Especially that. I did not want to mosey down to breakfast and chitchat with a retired schoolteacher/innkeeper, who wanted to serve me something-something muffins with homemade something on fancy something china. Forgive me. Going to that kind of place is a delight with you, but for now, just back from Gus's Laika Star, I want central heat and boring everydayness.

In any case, I have too much to absorb to risk social interaction with anyone. I want to be solitary for a day or two, and eat bowls of spicy chili in a sports bar, and watch the Celtics. Do you see how I depend on you to keep me from turning into a prototypical male?

A couple quick notes while they are fresh in my mind.

First, I made a call to the doctor Cindy recommended, and I will have a checkup tomorrow. Our health-care system may be the envy of the world, according to some politicians and talk-show hosts, but those blowhards never had to get an appointment in a strange town, without an insurance history in that office, and with an unspecified complaint. They should be forced to try it and the results should be played at their press conferences. Okay, that's my only political note.

So, doctor tomorrow.

I also called Kilkenny Charter Company. A young girl answered, maybe early teens from the sound of her voice, and she had atrocious phone manners. It took a few minutes, but I established that, no, her mom wasn't home, no, her mom might not be back tonight, no, Kilkenny Charter Company no longer existed. How dangerous, I couldn't help thinking, for a young girl to divulge to a complete stranger that her mother would not be home that night, and so forth. I suspect, though, that her telephone style had been cramped by people dunning them for back payment, because her voice became slightly steadier when she began to understand I wasn't calling to assert a claim. Although she hadn't been certain, Gus's Cindy had suggested that Kilkenny Charter had gone under after Paul's death. You can imagine the litigation and insurance adjusters descending on them. Long story short, I need to swing by there tomorrow and see what's what.

Then I dialed you. I called you at home, our home, and my fingers went over the numbers faster than I could have moved them consciously. Muscle memory. I have called you a thousand times from the road, sitting on the edge of motel beds, my eyes probably on a game. This time I heard the phone ring. Our ring. Halfway through the first ring I realized *she's not there* and I hung up almost as if I had done something wrong. But then I hit redial, I'm not sure why, and I listened to the phone ring in our old house. Fatigue, probably, but I started to choke up, imagined the sound of the phone passing through the house, touching your studio, the pictures of Paul in his lacrosse uniform, the pictures of your parents' wedding, the houseplants, the chipped cookie jar. Everything. Then suddenly your voice answered. Of course, it was merely a recording, and I listened to it more carefully than anything I can remember. My girl. My Hadley. As I listened, I had a flushed feeling. I wondered what we are doing, where we are going, why are we so far apart? And now you tell me we are on a docket for a final decree, and that developers have put a bull's-eye on our orchard. I am concerned, if it comes to it, that you will strap yourself to the bulldozer blade to prevent them from cutting into our land. And I don't think I am kidding. You know I will stand with you and any decision regarding the house. It's haunted, I suppose, but only by good days.

After hearing your voice, I came within a whisker of calling your cell, but then I decided no, stay with the plan. Is it a plan? Are you okay that way? I don't know how else to say it: these letters are the best therapy we've ever undergone. I remember that horrible marriage counselor we went to see, Dr. Ames, and she kept secretly checking the time on her wristwatch, and she wore those hideous calfskin boots, and it became clear she knew less about everything in the world than we did. You said on the way out, "We shouldn't pay for dumb," and as mixed up as we were right then, I still had to laugh. In any case, I can hear you in these letters. I can see you. The back and forth has slowed us down in important ways. If you're okay with it, indulge me a little longer.

Let me take a break here. I need to eat and I need to rest for a little. I should tell you that I am sitting at the little motel table—the round top they provide for business dopes like me who are supposed to find this all, gee whiz, just great—and I am writing, as you can see, on motel stationery. The stationery is surprisingly rich, again as you can see. I realized, though, that when you turn the TV off in a motel room the decorations become absolutely absurd. It's as if the TV is the only window in the place, and if you don't stare at it you are reminded that you are residing in someone's idea of a neutral, deliberately impersonal adult bedroom. Still, it's okay for a few nights. And the Celtics are on at ten.

* * *

It's late night and I can't sleep. The Celtics lost, by the way, and looked feeble doing it. My cough has kicked in again and it feels like a rooted stump in my chest. I hope I don't sound like a hypochondriac, but I don't often feel lousy. I wish I could shake this. I'm sorry to bother you with it. I hope to get to the bottom of it tomorrow.

It's taken me most of the evening to get my mind around Julie's miscarriage. To know where and how to begin thinking about it. It is a piece of the puzzle that we had been missing, isn't it? You and Julie both put your fingers on the source of Paul's reaction, I imagine: he loved too much. It was his one vulnerability, although I'm uncertain you can ever call a loving nature a true vulnerability. But he opened himself, I suspect is what we all mean, and he gave himself to an idea like no one I ever met. I can easily picture him absolutely embracing the child, the potential life, and casting his mind forward to the moment the baby arrived. A child, Hadley. Our grandchild. I would give anything to have met that child. I know you feel the same.

The other part of me, the more worldly and tired part, guards against making things too neat. No question, I'm sure, the miscarriage threw him, but I'm not positive we can draw too many conclusions from it. We both learned long ago that A doesn't necessarily follow B, and to pretend it does now would be unfair to Paul. He was a complex, incredibly thoughtful young man. I think he loved Julie deeply, and yet, yet . . . he still went away, didn't he? He still planned to go north, to leave Amherst, to allow her to slip out of his life. I would never say that to Julie, and I am entirely pleased she has a big, hearty football player from Michigan in her life, but I don't feel the perspective over this particular hill has given me the view for which I hoped. Why did Paul leave her when she had suffered such a setback? Wouldn't such an event have brought them closer together instead? I don't know. I have no clear insight. I just have threads of ideas and possibilities and I am wary of tugging too hard on any individual line of reasoning. (Your unraveling sweater notion, I guess.) I try to imagine that boy on the plane as he left to travel north for a year, and I attempt to climb into his thoughts and I discover I can't. We are all unknowable, aren't we?

I feel I don't know my son right now. The feeling will pass, I'm sure, but that's how I feel in this lonely motel tonight.

You know, I haven't mentioned your seeing the northern lights, because it seems so uncanny, and so unlikely, that I wondered if you could have been seeing things. How strange, really, that we would have seen the same event from different sides of the continent. I suppose a physicist or astronomer could explain the phenomenon, but I don't care to hear it. Call it a sign. Call it a freak chance that both of us could see such a thing so many miles apart. Add to that the fact that I stood watching them a day away from Paul's crash site, and I hardly know what to make of it.

I am going to try to sleep now. I'm sending you all good thoughts. I will write tomorrow to let you know what Mrs. Kilkenny has to report. Before I forget, I wanted to thank you for the sketches you have included in your letters. I study them, you know. I know the artist pretty well.

Sam

December 19

H—

Lord, do I have a story to tell. Remember when one or the other of us would come home with some juicy insight or dollop of gossip—okay, so we are as venal as the next couple—and we would pour two whiskeys and get near a fire and the deal was the other person could *only* ask questions about the ongoing story? No interruptions, no everyday jazz about dentists or what we might have for dinner. The story hour. Well, I have center stage right now and you will die to hear this story.

You didn't know you were married—still married, I might add—to a first-rate detective. Here goes.

I have this theory, as you know, that 11 a.m. is the optimal hour for catching someone on the phone or in person. Any earlier and the person is still in breakfast mode. Later, the person is out doing chores or tracking down lunch. Most of the world's business, I swear, takes place between 11:00 and 11:30. After that it's a crap shoot.

So at 9 I rented a car, and at 10:50 I was at the former headquarters of Kilkenny Charter Company. Picture a plane hangar, really just an oversized Quonset hut, next to a wide lake. The script of *Kilkenny Charter* had long since faded away to ghost letters, and on one side of the hangar high school kids had spray-painted the usual teen hieroglyphics. The place appeared deserted. I've read enough mystery novels to know how to case a joint, so I sat in my car and drank Dunkin' Donuts coffee and waited. I didn't have an appointment, remember, but I had told the girl on the phone the night before that I would swing by and I imagined the message would have been delivered. So I was doing a Sam Spade imitation out in my car, trying to remain inconspicuous as I watched the place.

Eleven, nothing. Eleven twelve, she shows up. She drives an old Chevy pickup, sky blue, and it has plenty of brown patches of rust. She climbs out, slides out, actually, because she is extremely short. She wears a man's leather bomber jacket, jeans, and a plain black watch cap. She hurries around the side and fishes a key out of her jacket. Door open, door shut. Obviously there is some sort of office around front.

I'm not sure why, but I felt wary of Mrs. Kilkenny. I couldn't quite figure why she would want to contact me after all this time. Surely anything she had of Paul's, or any information she had about the accident, had already been wrung out of her by the authorities. I felt a con coming on, and I admit I was almost amused by the possibility. Maybe that's strange, I don't know, but there it is.

I waited another five minutes, then went around to the office. You can picture that, too. Disheveled, paper everywhere, schoolteacher metal desks, camel bells that rattle when you push through the door. Parts and odd pieces of aviation equipment around the dooryard, most of it covered with snow now.

Mrs. Kilkenny was on her hands and knees, feeding a small flame in a woodstove as I stuck my head inside. She looked up, said nothing, and went back to feeding the fire. Who knows what she thought, but I admired her sangfroid.

"Mrs. Kilkenny?" I asked.

"Who's asking?" she said.

(She *actually* said that, a line straight out of an Ed McBain novel.)

I gave her my name.

"Let me just get this going," she said. "Cold as the devil."

She rocked back on her knees. The fire snapped a little. She burned paint sticks. Then she tossed in a few pieces of pine tinder and the fire died for a second, then sprang back. She closed the door of the stove and didn't move. She listened to the stove and in a few more moments she opened the door and tossed in a fair-sized log. I couldn't feel any heat from the stove. A picture window looked out on the water.

"I'd offer you coffee," she said, standing, "but I just arrived myself. Sorry."

"That's okay," I said, raising my Dunkin' Donuts coffee. "I have mine."

"So you do," she said.

We waited for the heat. Or something. She appeared profoundly uncomfortable. She had said nothing about Paul. No customary "Gee, glad to meet you, so sorry about your son." But then again, I hadn't said anything about the loss of her husband. So I did. Said I was sorry. Said I had been out to the plane wreck. That's what I was doing in Alaska. And so forth.

She was a tough little plug, believe me. It became clear as I talked that she was never going to say she was sorry about our son. Do you know that kind of person? She wasn't going to give an inch, because her entire life rested on the edge of a cliff, every day, and she couldn't take a deep breath without worrying that the exhalation would blow her to oblivion. And here was this man who caused her pain—that's how she saw it, believe me—by daring to have a son who happened to be on a plane when her husband crashed it. Who had hired the plane, in fact. I was one more thing the world did to her.

She asked me to sit. I did. The stove started pushing more heat. My mind raced around, trying to figure her angle, but then I decided to watch it like a piece of theater. I knew she had a role to play, and so I contented myself to watch and listen. She didn't disappoint.

"What would you think," she asked, "if I had some information that put things in a whole different light?"

"Information about what?"

She inclined her head. She was reluctant to say anything specific.

"About the crash?" I asked.

She nodded again.

"I'm not sure what you mean," I said.

"If I told you that things might not be as they appear, what would you say to that?"

"You're going to have to give me more to go on," I said.

The stove by this time had started to warm the place. She pushed back in her desk chair. I suspected she didn't want to meet my eyes when she said the next thing.

"What if I told you your son wasn't on the plane that day?"

I expected a million things, but never that. Choose your cliché: you could have knocked me over with a feather, or whatever it is people say when they get a shock. I stared at her. I drank some coffee. Not for a second did I think it could possibly be true, but this woman had more nerve than I had estimated. I gave her a careful nod.

"Say again?" I said, which is an old expression my grandmother used to employ when she didn't understand something. She came from Tennessee. I hadn't used that expression in years.

"What if your son hadn't been on that plane?" she said. "Would that be a thing worth knowing?"

"Who was it then?"

"A boy about your son's age. But not your son."

"This sounds a little desperate on your part, you know."

"They do an autopsy?"

"No," I said. "No point to it."

"That's right," she said. "It was my husband, all right. But your son wasn't with him."

Her plan folded out easily from that point. I admit I was fascinated. You may feel a little furious reading this, sweetheart, but you shouldn't. Think of a pale spider on a pine hedge, spinning for flies or insects. That's all she was. She had hatched this plan in a feeble attempt to extort us. If I paid her ten thousand dollars, she would tell me where he went. If not, this conversation never happened and I could believe anything I liked. She didn't really give a damn, she said. She was selling the business and heading down to Idaho, and her husband had died, true enough, and he hadn't been such great shakes to begin with. She could use the money, she didn't deny that, but our son, she said, had gone into hiding. Some men do, she said. Some women, too. They decide they don't like the way their lives have gone, and things feel so piled up that they figure it's easier to burn it down and rebuild than try to remodel.

You have to hand it to her, honey. As deplorable as her tactics were, for the smallest instant she had me going. What if Paul had decided at the last minute to do something different? What if he *had* run off somewhere, establishing himself in a new life? I knew it was absurd, but I also know the human heart does crazy things at times.

Good sense—reality—reasserted itself. I told her I appreciated her offer, but if Paul still walked the earth no power in the world could keep us all apart. She smiled and said you never know. I told her you do know. I told her I know. I told her my wife knows. Then I left her.

Driving back to the motel, I felt I had been locked in a room with a small, feral animal. I don't mean that to be overly cruel. But her humanity had slipped away by circumstances, and what remained was simply appetite and worry. She reminded me of a pound dog, the type that no one will adopt, the type that walks back and forth in its enclosure and is the source of its own misery—though the world has done horrible things to it—but it cannot still itself long enough to accept kindness. Neither did any conscience remain. Our son's death, the rent, repair bills for the planes— they no longer differentiated themselves in her mind.

Okay, last subject. No worries, really, but the doctor didn't like the sound of my chest. He suspects pneumonia. Knows it is. I confess he's probably right and it is almost a relief to give in to it. He said I will feel better soon if he gets the right medicine pumping through me. I haven't stopped coughing in a while, and it will be a mercy to draw a decent breath.

I am thinking of you. Our last business is finished on Paul's behalf. Now we have to trust in time.

Sam

December 22

Sam,

I am on my way to you. Made arrangements for Turner and Rosie to look after Cat, left the island at first light—didn't even wait for the *Laura B*, but got Turner to take me to Port Clyde in his lobster boat. He arranged for me to catch a ride to Portland with Jim Nealy from the co-op, and I was able to get a flight to New York. I'm on the plane now, and hoping to connect with an Alaska Air flight to Anchorage this afternoon.

So much to say to you, but my hands are shaking. I've tried calling your motel, and you're registered, but you're never in the room. I'm in shock at what you wrote. Paul . . . is it possible? I'm afraid to fly right now. It's completely crazy, but I'm terrified the plane will crash before I have the chance to see him—and you—again.

My mind is spinning. Did I dream your letter?

Is this *all* a dream?

H.

Dear Sam,

I'm writing into the void. Where are you? There was no answer in your room, all the times I tried you on the road between the boat and the Portland airport. I tried you from JFK, and even had the manager slide a message under the door to have you call my cell if you came in—but now we're in the air, all electronics turned off, with a seven-hour flight ahead of me, and I don't know where you are. I'm so glad to be writing to you right now, anyway. To hold on to that.

Wondering about all of it, I'm losing my mind. Are you even sicker than you've told me—have you gone to the hospital? I've never felt so out of control in my life. My thoughts are racing. I find myself thinking of Mrs. Kilkenny, of what she meant. And then I think—but we saw him, we identified his body. And then—oh, Sam, you must be thinking it, too—there was so little, really, to identify. What came back to us from the crash, that wasn't Paul. Trying to pull it together now, I'll try to keep writing. I'll hand you a sheaf of letters when I get to Alaska. The simple things, just forcing myself to breathe and stay sane.

I've got a window seat, right in front of the wing, and we're flying west into the sunset. There's snow on the ground below, and the lakes in western New York are frozen, and everything is orange, butterscotch, from the setting sun. The pilot warned of chop over Lake Erie, and indeed we're just flying out of a turbulent stretch.

I'm still shaking, but not as badly as before. I'm thinking of what I'm flying to, and it's got me careening between panic and ecstasy. I feel as if I'm levitating. Then I close my eyes and think of how shocking this all is, and I feel as if I'm going down in flames.

Taking this seat, I caught sight of a young family behind me. A mother, father, and little boy have the wing seats, and I had the strongest, wildest memory of flying with Paul. When he was—what, four? five?—you told him that flying over the wing was the most comfortable, stable place to sit on a plane, and nothing else would ever do again. He always took your word; it always became gospel for him.

I'm surrounded by people right now. That family in the seats just behind, and a couple sitting next to me, many of them part of a tour group on their way to the Alaska Railroad, some sort of train trip to see the snowfields and the northern lights. I'm overhearing conversations about Talkeetna and Fairbanks, and the flight attendant just came to ask what I want to drink, and I can barely think or speak. I just want to sit here, write to you, and ask if it is real.

I know you say Mrs. Kilkenny isn't believable. But Sam! *Could Paul be alive?* Okay, I'm up in the air, it's like a time capsule, far from anything in my ordinary life. Maybe I'll rip this up before I hand it to you, if I ever find you, if you ever return to your room at the Fairtown Motel—or maybe I won't. Right now, my grip on the pen, and the sight of my handwriting on this sheet of paper, are the only things holding me together.

My son, my boy, my baby ... You have no idea what it's done to me. What do I even mean by that? Losing him? Or that he might be alive? All of it, ripping me up, as if I'm being clawed from the inside out. I'm indulging myself here—you'll never see this letter, so I'm just going to go for it.

He was in my body. You and I made love, and we made Paul. And I know there was never any doubt, not for a moment or a second, that you wanted him and loved and adored him—but you don't know what it was to have him living inside you, Sam. From the moment we conceived him—I knew. I felt him there, and not just the biological fact of an embryo, but his soul. I felt the Paul he was—the little boy, the good man—all of it right then, that very first instant.

And we were together—nine months. Every breath, we took it together. Every beat his heart pumped, I felt it. My blood was his blood. And then he was born—I won't even ask if you remember. I know that was the day of days for both of us—hard labor, I went through it, but I don't take credit—you were there with me, and I couldn't have done it without you, not the way we did it—that zone I got into, pain and bliss and clarity, and then Paul in my arms—you handing him to me. I don't remember the doctor, the nurse, the midwife, none of them—I only remember you and Paul. We were three, we were one another, we were our family.

But still . . . in some ways, he was mine alone. I know you understand. He was in me. His body lived in mine. So that's why I've felt, well . . . frozen. As if without him in my life, in my sphere, nothing mattered or made sense anymore, and I was something like the Tin Man—frozen in place and time. This isn't new to you—I've tried to explain it many a time, even in our letters this fall. Here's the thing, though—I was frozen, not dead. I was like one of those intrepid, sad explorers who traverse the Jasper ice fields and fall into a crevasse. They don't freeze to death all at once; they might be upside down or sideways, but they're still alive, just caught in the ice.

That's been me. Sam, is this just wishful thinking—am I a Monday morning quarterback, looking back at the game, trying to make sense of what I felt by what I now know? Because I know so much more now! I know that some lady, a short strange lady who gave you a bad vibe, name of Mrs. Kilkenny, dressed in a brown bomber jacket, says that Paul is alive.

THAT'S WHAT SHE SAID.

I know you think she was conning you, all that about the spider spinning the web, and the ten thousand dollars and all, but SAM!! Here's the truth—I know she's right, I know he wasn't on that plane. Think back to that moment when we identified his body—just think, Sam. We believed it was him because we were told he was on the plane. But he wasn't. He's alive. Those remains belonged to some other poor soul . . .

And here's how I know—I FEEL IT. Haven't you read a million stories, seen a million movies, about people, and they're usually mothers, who say they would *know* if someone they loved was dead? Their child. They'd feel it—in their own bodies, in their skin, deep in their bones. Well, I've never felt that. Not at all, Sam. I've felt frozen, it's true, and I've wanted to stay numb. But I've never felt his death inside me.

And that's what I'm going on. I'm on this plane, desperately worried about you—why you're not answering your phone in the motel room, why the manager seemed so evasive when I asked—actually demanded, and okay, at the top of my lungs—that he slide that note under the door for you. I can barely stand it, here in my window seat, two rows ahead of the wing, bouncing up and down in rocky air as the pilot keeps the seat belts–fastened light on and as the plane gains altitude as we try to find a smoother path. I'm frantic with worry over you.

But I'm also—God help me, truly—beside myself with joy. Because here's what I think. Not hope—*think*. I think you're with Paul. You came to your senses, and cashed in whatever it took to get ten thousand dollars to pay Mrs. Kilkenny. She's not scary, she's not a con—she's an angel. That's where my thoughts are going.

You gave her the money, and she told you where our boy is. She gave you directions, or a map, or GPS coordinates. You walked or drove or flew or crawled to wherever he is. And why ever he's there—it doesn't matter. He's our sweet, sensitive boy. The trauma of Julie losing the baby—that has to be it. He had a breakdown. Maybe he had to go live alone in nature for a while. That would be our boy, wouldn't it? Maybe he had to ford the river and climb the mountain and live in the shadows all by himself, to heal his heart.

Sweetheart, wouldn't that be Paul?

And you've gone to him. I pray, and I haven't turned to God in years, not since Paul's been gone . . . that you are well. That you've healed enough to take the journey in safety. Your lungs are fine, your fever is down, your heart is steady . . . Your mind is clear, and you're going to save our son, bring him home.

Back when I still believed—as I do again—one of my favorite prayers was by Thomas Merton. Remember when I went on that retreat, down to the Abbey of Gethsemani in Kentucky, outside Bardstown, in the smoky hills filled with bourbon distilleries—back when Paul was little, when being a mother, as much as I loved it, took me away from myself, from my own heart, and from my painting—and I went down to the abbey to connect with the Holy Spirit? I chose that place because it's where Thomas Merton had lived and written.

And I loved Merton. He was a Trappist monk—and you know the Trappists are the marines of religious life. They're rigorous and devoted, up at three each morning to go to chapel, and he was a poet and scholar, and I loved the place. It was spring, and there were monks in silence, and chants through the hours, and redbuds and dogwoods in bloom all along the woodland paths. And although Merton had died years earlier, I felt inspired by his presence—by the fact that he had once loved a woman, a nurse he'd met while in the hospital in Louisville . . . he'd written her letters right there at the abbey. He'd called her "M."

That made him so human to me. I felt that a monk who'd fallen in love, who'd felt the pull of desire—away from his religious vows, straight into the love affair that he and M had, short as it may have been—would understand a young mother who adored her husband and son more than air and sunshine, yet needed to escape those bonds for a time, felt she needed to regain her mind, life, and ability to paint.

I found Merton's prayer on that trip, and I used to say it every day—and I find myself saying it now, as I fly west toward you and Paul, toward Mrs. Kilkenny's secret, toward Alaska. It's almost Christmas. All these people are flying there for a special holiday event—they want to see the Aurora Borealis on Christmas Eve. Something like the star, I guess.

I love Merton's words—about trusting God "though I may seem to be lost and in the shadow of death." It speaks to worst fear. The dread, the demon, the darkness, death itself—everything we fear most. That's where we've been, in the shadow of Paul's death—all three of us. You, me, and Paul. But we're not now. We're not now.

Soon we'll be together.

The little boy with the seat over the wing just ran up the aisle—he'd gone to the bathroom with his father. The seat belt sign is still on, but the flight attendant let them get up, and even though the plane is bouncing like a ship on high seas, the boy seems so happy. He loves flying, just like Paul did. Remember when he was in second grade he read about flight, became obsessed with airplanes? We had to take him to the Outer Banks, to Kitty Hawk, to see where the first flight took place, and that was the year he named the chickens Wilbur and Orville. Two of the best laying hens we ever had . . .

He didn't die in a plane crash. He didn't, and you're with him now, and I'm halfway there, and soon we'll all be together.

H.

December 23

Dear Sam,

Am I a fool? I guess maybe I am. How can I look you in the eyes next time I see you? Now that we're both in Alaska, you might well ask why I'm writing you this letter instead of sitting at your bedside, bringing you tea and asking you to understand. Not that you blame me, at least not outwardly, and not that you want me to feel guilty. I'm doing that all on my own.

Seeing you yesterday, after traveling all day...maybe I wasn't at my best. Especially seeing you so sick. You completely played down how ill you are—I should have known from your letters, the fact that you'd checked into that motel, settled in really, when you had planned to be on the move. At least you were at the doctor's yesterday, getting some heavy-duty antibiotics, fighting him for wanting to put you into the hospital for a few days of IV treatment. You have pneumonia, an infection, and all I can think of is Jim Henson, the guy who invented the Muppets. How he got an infection and was *dead* in days. But you have a reprieve from my hovering because I was—and still am—completely blinded by the news about Paul.

I didn't want to fight with you yesterday—not after all we've been through, and not seeing you that way—and I know you want me to believe what you saw in Mrs.

Kilkenny's character (or, as you say, lack thereof). I realize you think it's saving me, us, future heartache. But . . . I'll get to that in a minute.

First, you. Seeing you after so long apart, I felt such a surge of emotion, of happiness, it nearly knocked me down. I can't believe you met my flight. When I told the motel manager my arrival time, it was just to give you fair warning. I really never meant for you to come to the airport, but I'm moved beyond words that you did.

That hug you gave me. Do you know, I can still feel it? I'll try to describe it for you. I came through the gate, tired and disoriented, bedraggled as hell after a day that started by crawling behind the woodpile to scoop up Cat—try catching a feral cat who doesn't want to be caught—then delivering her to Turner and Rosie's, crossing Muscongus Bay in near-gale conditions, continuing at that pitch the whole way to Alaska . . .

Arriving in Anchorage, looking around the baggage area for signs to ground transport, instead I saw you—gazing at me from across the floor, as if you'd held back a minute to watch me, maybe decide whether you wanted me there or not. I saw, and at first I thought it was hesitation, but then I realized it was something else—that smile of yours always gives you away. You were taking me in, the way I'd have done to you . . . you walked toward me, and the smile got bigger, and your eyes were gleaming. I guess I dropped my bags because my arms were suddenly open, and you were in them, and I felt your beard against my cheek, and I was afraid to turn my head because I didn't want you to know how much I wanted you to kiss me, but I didn't have to worry because suddenly I didn't have to think about anything, you were doing it all, kissing me. Holding me, and there we were, just rocking back and forth in the concourse of the Ted Stevens International Airport, and the hug was so deep I felt your heart against mine, and I felt your warmth in my bones.

Feel it still, I do, I do. In spite of how angry you are at me right now. Back to that in a minute.

You're so thin. I was shocked, once the reality of having your arms around me began to sink in. You were whispering to me, and I did hear what you said—and let me say right now, I felt and feel exactly the same way, even though I was too stunned or whatever to actually reply in words.

Your body felt lean and strong, and I know it's from mushing through the wilderness on the way to the crash site. You're all sinew, there's absolutely nothing extra, and that's what's got me crazed with worry right now. What are you living on? That cough is terrible, and so is the fact that you can't eat, and stop telling me you don't believe it's anything serious. I know you do. And as soon as I get back to Anchorage, I'm bundling you up and making you nothing but chicken soup.

For now I'm trusting that you're still in bed, where I left you. I still believe the adjoining rooms are best—we're both overwhelmed with the situation, and I don't want to confuse matters even more than they already are. But I slipped in this morning, curled up next to you, pressed against your back, trying to decide what to do. You were so mad last night, when I insisted that we pursue this thing—and I know you think you're right. But lying there in bed with you, for the first time in so long, I felt surer than I have about anything in years.

By now you've probably read the note I left you on the pillow ... so you know I was on my way to Kilkenny Charter Company. The cabdriver seemed oddly silent when I told him where I wanted him to take me. I pressed him, and he just said, "There are other charter companies if you want to go to Denali." When I asked what he meant, he just shook his head. Suddenly we were there—I saw the ghost letters on the side of the silver Quonset hut, and I stepped out of the car and felt the coldest wind I've ever felt in my life, and then he drove away and left me there.

And here I sit right now—waiting for someone to come to the desk. I'm in the room you described in your letter. There's the woodstove, right there. Crackling and spitting away, throwing very little heat. The place has an almost-abandoned feel. You did say Mrs. Kilkenney is selling the business—maybe that's done. But then why is the stove burning? I sit here on a torn black vinyl chair waiting to find out. And writing to you, hoping you're not too upset. And that you're feeling better ...

Sam, I have so much to tell you. It's two hours after I wrote that last part, and the entire world has just changed. First, oh help me, Paul is alive. I'll tell you all the details, but I'm on my way to him now. I am in stunned, overjoyed awe.

After I had waited for about twenty minutes, Eileen (that's her first name, Mrs. Kilkenny) walked into the office. I was pacing around, shivering, the woodstove barely throwing any warmth at all, and I could see my breath. She looked straight at me. This is the spookiest thing, and I can't possibly do it justice, but she knew just who I was.

"Mrs. West," she said. She had a glint in her eyes, and she said, "That day I met your husband, he said how much you loved your son. That's what he said. And I knew that meant you were coming. I knew you would have to come and hear what I have to say." Then she gestured for me to sit down, which I had to, because my knees were buckling.

I told her I was sorry about her husband, and she shrugged and pointed at a picture of him on the wall—you probably saw it. A cowboy, leaning against the strut of his plane—Stetson and all, and weathered face with the greatest grin ever, as if he loved being in the sky and was just raring to go up for another visit. I liked him. And in spite of your instincts, which are usually pretty dead-on, I liked her.

She poured me some strong coffee, offered to add a shot of Irish whiskey "for some holiday cheer." I said thanks anyway, but that she should go ahead—which she did. She told me to call her Eileen, and I said I was Hadley, and she said I was lucky to have caught her. She was just getting ready to clear out. Just as you said, she sold the business, and she and her daughter were heading to Idaho to spend Christmas with her sister.

I asked her to tell me everything she could about Paul. You're right about her being evasive. She talked around and around. How he'd been carrying too much stuff for the plane, they were over on the weight and he had to leave two bags behind.

And Sam, how at the last minute he was uncertain about leaving his luggage—so he changed his mind, let some other young man take his place. She said that during the busy season it's so hard to get a flight, the charter companies are booked up weeks, months in advance, and people jockey for planes.

I asked her what other young man, asked her to show me the manifest. That's when I saw the dishonesty you picked up on—she looked down, away, anywhere but at me. But then she stared straight into my eyes, dug into a box of papers she'd already packed. She pushed the register toward me and said,

"Your son's name is on the manifest, but he wasn't on the plane."

And I looked, and there in his handwriting was his name, Paul West . . . I nearly sobbed at the sight.

"That's why I need the money," she said. "Because... well, everything in this office hasn't always been so aboveboard. Let's say that not everyone who flew on a Kilkenny Charter filled out the proper paperwork. And once your son made up his mind not to fly, there was someone ready to take his seat..."

I came right out and asked her. "Drug dealer?"

She just shrugged again. "Don't ask, don't tell." Then she grinned, said we both—you and I, that is—must like mysteries, she could tell by the questions you'd asked as well. I couldn't respond because all I could think of was that Paul hadn't gotten on the plane, soon I'd know why and where he was, soon I'd be hugging him the way I hugged you this morning...

I heard her saying something about how she was going out on a big limb to tell me this, reveal the fact she'd broken federal aviation law by not filing proper documents... she'd reported Paul's name after the plane crashed, and she'd go to jail if the truth surfaced. I gather it wasn't the company's first offense.

So... that's when I called my lawyer. He started to try to talk me out of it, at least until we investigated further, but I wouldn't let him. It's the holidays, and everything will be closed, and besides—Eileen's flying down to see her sister. So he asked for her routing number, and I had him wire the money. Five thousand.

I still owe her another five, but she said she could tell I

was good for it. In fact, she said the two payments would work out in her favor—apparently any financial transactions ten thousand dollars or more are automatically reported to the IRS. She said she likes being "under the radar."

Okay, Sam. She didn't just tell me something—she gave me something. One of the bags that wouldn't fit on the plane. At first my heart sank—because I thought, well, if the reason Paul didn't get on the flight was because his baggage wouldn't fit, why wouldn't he have taken the bag? But she said it was because he had to hitchhike to where he was going, and he didn't want to carry it with him. He told her he'd be back.

She led me to the storage room—amazing what people leave behind. She said she'd sold most of it on eBay, but there were still a few things left. An old golf bag containing a few battered clubs, a fishing creel, a wicker picnic basket, a child's tricycle. And Paul's backpack. His faded purple one, Amherst colors, with the little orange key ring clipped to the strap. I could barely breathe, thought I might pass out. Eileen started to support me, but I gestured her away. I wanted to be alone with his things . . .

I opened it up—felt as if I were standing underwater. Pulled out his Block Island sweatshirt, a pair of worn-down Nike sneakers, a book of Gary Snyder poetry and Ken Kesey's *Sometimes a Great Notion*, and three *Sports Illustrated*s, each issue featuring an article by his father. Including his favorite, your interview with Muhammad Ali, where Ali repeated that quote: "Service to others is the rent you pay for your room here on earth." He'd said it once before, in a different interview, but you got him to explain his philosophy in a way that never stopped resonating with Paul. That underscored why he came north after losing the baby, why he was on his way to the village—he knew he had to serve others for a while.

There were other things—a notebook, a picture of Julie, one of me. One of Boing's fur mice. Did Paul really take that mouse with him, or did you stick it in as a joke for him to find later?

I admit being thrown by the fact he hasn't returned to Kilkenny's to pick up the pack, but wait till you hear where he went. You're not going to believe it—I'm in complete shock myself.

St. Luke's Abbey.

The Cistercians have a monastery in the native village Acush, on an island in Prince William Sound. He told Eileen he was going, and she helped him hitch a ride on a logging truck heading down to the ferry dock.

I'm on the ferry myself right now. Forgive my writing—the water is choppy, and the boat is bouncing on the waves. I'm in the cabin; it's very snug, and it comforts me to think of Paul taking this same voyage. I wanted to write you this letter instead of calling, because I know you'd try to get out of bed and come with me. I wish my motives were completely selfless—that I could tell you I'm thinking only of you and your health—but the truth is not so straightforward.

I need to go there by myself, Sam. How do I say this? I want to believe so badly. She seemed honest—she has to be, right? There's no way a person—a mother herself—could get our hopes up like this if the story were untrue. Part of me wants to protect you from disappointment if he's not there. And if he is—which I have to believe—then I'll find him and call you. It's a more personal form of Pascal's wager. Act "as if." We have no way of knowing whether Eileen told the truth and Paul is at the abbey, but I'm impelled toward him as if he himself were calling for me. Nothing could keep me from taking this trip.

Something else drives me as well. I told you that after so many years of no-faith, no-belief, I started praying again. I felt a bolt, a connection with God. All my childhood faith came flooding back, and more; memories of that visit to Gethsemani, in Kentucky...when I felt such peace and found my own heart and self again. And you know, the Trappists are Cistercians as well...it's an ancient order, and it seems like no coincidence that Paul found his way to their only outpost in Alaska, especially after the trauma of losing the baby.

Right now I feel as if we're in the middle of a miracle. It's almost Christmas—two more days. I'm so focused on Paul, I'd almost forgotten. You're not religious, but you've always been so spiritual. You've always found meaning and beauty in love, nature, poetry, even in the grace you see in sports. We've been led here for a reason—to Alaska, this icy land, this place I'd thought had stolen our son, taken his life. And now it's going to give him back.

It's already given me back my love for you, for us. We have each other again, and soon we'll have Paul. Rest well, Sam . . . get better and know that we will see you soon.

Hadley

December 23

Dearest Hadley—

You are mine, aren't you? It feels almost like a dream. And I am yours, never to leave again. That's decided and it was always inside us. What fools we've been—what a reckless thing we almost did.

I'm writing this sitting up in bed. My cough is better and I feel stronger by the hour. I don't hate you, Hadley, for going to where you believe Paul must be. I love you for it. I worry that what you discover will break your heart. And it's my heart now, again, always, and I need it whole and strong.

I want to return your gift of poetry with a poem that I love. And I will. It is the saddest poem in the English language, one that is five hundred years old. It is about the death of a son and I found it shortly after Paul's death. I didn't share it with you before because it is a father's poem for the death of his son. You'll understand when you read it. I'll close with it. Right now I am thinking of you, and your brave search, and I am sending you my love to protect you. But of course my love can't protect you, as much as we would like to believe such things. We know that now. We know it more deeply, more truly than we can know anything. Our love could not protect Paul; his love could not protect

Julie. Love is not a shield, or a guard. It's the hand we give to each other, and we cannot live our lives holding on for balance. But the hand is there, waiting and willing the return, and the hand is never quite at rest without the other.

I am getting mushy. I blame it on the medicine. Maybe I am still a little tired.

It's silly to be writing this, of course, but these letters brought us back together. So this is my last to you. I am writing it to tell you how I love you, how your body fits mine, how what has been broken is now mended. It is not a seamless repair; I wouldn't want it to be. We are dented, scraped, more fragile than before. I wouldn't trade those marks of our life together. We should never be afraid of them or embarrassed by them. I am proud that we did not let go. Perhaps it is Paul's last gift to us, our son, who in his goodness reminded us of our own.

This is your quest, Hadley. I cannot bring myself to believe Paul is alive, dearest. You are alone in that, and I would not for a moment permit my cynicism to color your search. He was your heart and I cannot ask you not to follow him.

So much has happened in such a short time. Let me just tell you what I thought when you came through the gate at the airport. Would it surprise you to know that for the slightest instant I didn't recognize you? A heartbeat, no more. Maybe that was the slight hesitation you observed. Then— you will think I am crazy—I saw you. But I saw you as I never have before. You were that college girl I met and courted so many years ago, the young mother who gave me a son, my lover, my mate, my friend, my enemy, my joy. Although the movies always portray such moments as high drama, that was not how I felt. I experienced, instead, a flush of pure contentment, pure knowledge that this person belongs in my life, and will always, and that we will not be separated again unless fate takes one of us. The metaphors are lousy—like an old friend, a slipper, a well-worn pair of jeans. Those images make my vision of you sound farcical and shopworn. No, you were the rising from the bed after illness, the garden loaded with fresh seed, the window wiped clean and fresh with vinegar and old newspaper. The sun in the window, the clock ticking, the jay calling, the kettle whistling. Everything, Hadley, and small things, and big things, and all things. That was your return to me.

I have canceled the adjoining room.

We have started to begin again, as some poet or songwriter said somewhere.

Okay, the poem. It will make you sad. I found it in an old college textbook down in the basement some gloomy Sunday and I did not understand it at first. The opening two lines pierced me and I have kept them in my mind since Paul has been gone. Ben Jonson, a contemporay of Shakespeare's, wrote it at the death of his seven-year-old son, Benjamin. It begins with him saying goodbye not only to his son, but to joy . . . all joy forevermore:

Farewell, thou child of my right hand, and joy;
My sin was too much hope of thee, loved boy.

Then he says God lent him the child. The child died precisely on his seventh birthday . . .

Seven years thou wert lent to me, and I thee pay,
Exacted by thy fate, on the just day.

It concludes, sweetheart, by wishing his child soft peace. And he says in the final couplet that he, Ben Jonson, hopes never to risk his heart so profoundly again:

For whose sake henceforth all his vows be such
As what he loves may never like too much.

Jonson wrote the poem in 1616 and you can hear the agony still. I loved Paul in every way a father can love a son. But I am not going with Jonson and abandoning my hope to love again. I will not say goodbye to love. Not while you are here. Not while you remain my wife.

Sam

December 24

Dear Sam,

Paul was at the monastery.

That said, you were right about Eileen Kilkenny...I didn't want you to be, but you were. She timed it well, too; I'm sure she's far from Anchorage by now. I wonder if there's really a sister in Idaho. I don't suppose it matters. You're at the Fairtown Motel, I'm on yet another island, in a different ocean, at St. Luke's Abbey. The winds of Prince William Sound howl at the door. Except for chanting the hours, the monks here keep silence...they live like the early Desert Fathers, only instead of hot and arid desert sands, the land here lies buried beneath snow and ice.

How do I tell you this? I know now that Paul is dead. I finally feel it, in a way I never could before. Surrounded by ice, everything in me has thawed. I couldn't take that journey to the crash site as you did, with so much strength and courage. But I'm here in the far country where he died, and I feel his death. Because of a con woman, as motivated as she was by greed, I've been led to this place. Eileen did me a favor.

I'm embraced by the wind and the feeling of more snow on the way, and the sound of the deep voices echoing from the chapel. It's vespers, dark outside, candles burning in the windows. From my very spare room on the second floor I look outside, across a bare courtyard, and see silhouettes of the monks bowing in prayer. They know my story—I told the abbott—so I know they are praying for us. For Paul.

Let me start at the beginning of my time here, tell you how I learned what I know. By the time I arrived on the island, late in the afternoon, I was even more churned up than before. Partly because of the ferry crossing—against the tide, and there were ice floes in the harbors at both ends of the trip, drifts bumping the steel hull as I sat in the cabin writing to you. It made me feel better, connected, writing you and imagining that Paul had been on the boat before me.

There was a strong headwind. We had to angle into the island dock, and as I stood at the foot of the stairs on the vessel deck, I watched as the ferry's bow reared up and down and up and down on the slate-gray sea before the crew members were able to finally, successfully throw the line to guys waiting on the dock. By the time I stepped onshore, I had such sea legs and was so overtaken by the idea of having started this journey at sea in the Atlantic, finishing it in the Pacific, on my way to find my lost son, my lost family, I was weeping, and I nearly kissed the ground. It's true, Sam... I've been at sea. We both have, my love.

A monk met the boat. He had a heavy work coat on over his cowl, his robe. Seems that the monks make cheese and fruit preserves, and he had a truckload of boxes to send over to the mainland. I watched him lift the cartons into the ferry's hold, my heart pounding as I wondered whether he knew Paul, trying to gauge his age, which seemed to me about thirty.

I tried to imagine Paul as a monk. I stared at the young man, watching him finish loading. He saw me there, came to me with a big smile on his face as if he knew I was waiting for him. He walked over to me, said hello. And I couldn't do anything but say, "I'm looking for my son."

"Your son?" he asked.

"Paul West," I said.

"I don't know that name," he said. He had such kindness in his eyes, as if he knew I had come a long way to ask about Paul, but he didn't rush to fill the silence or ask me questions that might lead to a happier answer. And the strange thing was, I didn't feel let down or disappointed or even slightly deterred. I was still holding on to Eileen's words, her sureness about Paul's destination being the abbey. I suppose I was thinking that maybe Paul had taken a religious name. Perhaps he had changed his identity, been led to let go of his old self, his old name. I didn't care if or why he'd done such a thing—I just wanted to find him.

"I'll take you to the monastery," the monk said simply, opening the door of his pickup truck, helping me in. I was clutching Paul's knapsack, and I saw his eyes light on it. This is strange, but in that single glance, I felt he saw everything: saw me, saw you, saw Paul, saw our lives together, saw the endless love I have for you and our son.

He drove in silence, but it's funny—he had the radio on, a rock station playing the kind of indie music Paul liked, and I couldn't help but smile to think of this young man taking religious vows but still liking Morrissey and Coldplay, and all those bands Paul listened to. After a few miles I asked him his name.

"Brother Matthew," he said.

"Where are you from?" I asked.

"Bellingham, Washington, originally," he said.

"And was your name always Matthew?"

He shook his head and smiled. "I was born Jason. But that's not a monk's name."

"Thomas Merton was called Father Louis after he became a priest," I said.

"You know Merton?" he asked, and his eyes lit up. I nodded and smiled, because my point had been made—twice. Men sometimes changed their names when they joined the Trappists.

"How long have you been a monk?" I asked.

"I came to the abbey right out of college," he said. He glanced over. "How old is Paul?"

"He would be twenty-three," I said.

"Would be?" he asked, catching me.

"Is," I said.

"He's . . . you think he's here?" he asked.

"Yes," I said. I wanted to describe him, ask Brother Matthew if he'd seen him, but something made me keep it to myself. I'm not sure why, but suddenly my voice wouldn't work. We'd entered a village, and I stared out the window at the houses and buildings. It was a poor place—trailers and ramshackle cabins, some of them with satellite dishes in the yards, rusty cars parked at odd angles, smoke wisping out of every chimney into the opaque gray sky. We passed what was obviously a school—a square brick building with children's pictures taped to the windows—and the town square, with a tall totem pole rising—it had to be thirty feet—with such fierce faces carved into the wood. At the very top was a bald eagle with a sharp beak, eyes painted bright red. The sight of that eagle filled me with fear—it reminded me that this is a brutal land.

And suddenly we turned up the long snowy drive to the monastery. I climbed out of the truck, followed Brother Matthew toward the abbey—a big spare structure, you'd never guess it was a church from the outside except for the simple black cross on the roof. I stared up at it, in such stark contrast to the darkening twilight snow sky, and while I was standing there, two things happened.

The door opened, and an old monk walked out. He was tall and very thin, and he gazed at me long and hard with bright blue eyes. I was transfixed by his expression—he looked as if he'd been waiting for me. I saw Brother Matthew say something to him, then heard the young man say good-bye to me, and felt the old monk take my hands. He stood very still, staring at me with such kindness, my eyes filled spontaneously with tears. I opened my mouth to ask about Paul, when the second thing happened.

An owl flew by.

A snowy owl, pure white, and so close I could feel the tips of its wings brush the top of my head, and even in the falling darkness see the yellow eyes. Its talons were extended, and as I stood there watching, it swooped down the far side of a small hill and disappeared. My tears were already flowing, and imagining that owl bringing death to whatever creature it was hunting made them come harder.

"Come in," the old monk said, leading me into the church. We walked through the nave, through a heavy wooden door into the attached guesthouse. He had me sign a register, and I felt him watching me as I turned the pages back, back... three years ago. I read all the entries during the weeks that Paul might have first arrived.

"You're looking for someone?" he asked.

I nodded, but didn't speak.

None of the names looked familiar, I didn't recognize any of the handwriting. But then, turning one more page, I saw it: his name, his real name, Paul West. And the date: the day before he would have gotten on that plane.

"My son!" I said.

"You're Paul's mother?" he asked.

"Yes," I said. "Where is he?"

The old man looked back at me with such compassion— and I can't tell you what that did to me. It turned my heart to ice, because he was telling me how sorry he was, how final this was. Still, I wasn't able to accept anything but the possibility that Paul was here, at the abbey, on the island, in the enclosure with the other monks.

"I need to see him."

"My name is Frederic," he said. "I am the abbot of St. Luke's . . . and was, three years ago, when Paul came for a night."

"A night . . ."

"Yes," he said. "He was on his way to begin a life teaching the Inuits, and he came here to the monastery."

"To join the order?" I whispered.

"No, Mrs. West," he said. "To spend a night in silence, to reflect on . . . well, on his life."

"Did he tell you that?"

He nodded, and I think I saw him grappling with how much to reveal to me. Had Paul confided in him, made a confession? I don't know, and he didn't tell me. But he said something I'll never forget, and I wish you had been with me to hear it, to see his eyes as he spoke of our son.

"He was filled with love," the abbot said. "For this life, for the world, for where he had come from and where he was going. He spoke of his parents, of the goodness in your home. And how he knew he had to take that forth."

"Forth?"

"To the village," he said. "Where he would have taught."

"You know he didn't make it there?" I asked, something already sinking in, and as crazy as this sounds, Sam—the idea, the acceptance, coming in sideways, into my consciousness as if through a dream.

"Yes. I read the news account of the plane crash a few days later."

I waited for him to say he was sorry for my loss, but instead he took my hands again, as he had outside the abbey. He stared into my eyes with that same compassion, wordless and ineffable. The depth of his love was ... Sam, it was like nothing you've ever imagined. I felt as if my own father were holding my hands, telling me that my son was with him now. That's how it felt.

I cried, of course. The abbot let me, didn't say anything or try to stop me. I wept, and I thought, oddly, of Eileen Kilkenny. She must have needed money badly to do what she did.

She gave us a gift. Sending me here to look for Paul—did she have any idea that I would in fact find him? Because I have. Abbot Frederic led me up the guesthouse stairs, to this room—the same one Paul stayed in the night before he took that flight.

Paul slept in this little bed, his gaze fell upon the single chair, the plain wood cross on the whitewashed wall. Our son came here, as the abbot said, to reflect. And wasn't that Paul, Sam? Can't you imagine him seeking out this beautiful place, offering his grief over the baby, his love and his hopes and even his fears and dreams, to the monks, the pines, the ice, the snowy owl?

Sam, you knew...you felt it, felt our son's death and knew that his body was no longer here in the world, when you left our picture there at the plane, where our beautiful boy died. I had to come to this place of ice and snow and austere beauty to feel his death myself, and to get you back. No, that's wrong—to get *us* back.

What do we do now?

I think I know. I'm not going to mail this letter. I'm going to carry it with me, along with Paul's backpack (which of course he never would have left behind, not with Julie's picture or your articles, not unless he absolutely had to) when I return to Anchorage tomorrow morning. Abbot Frederic said there is a predawn ferry, for the residents who work in town, and I will be on it. He promised me that Brother Matthew will drive me back to you. "Paul's father," as he put it. I hope that you will still be sleeping, and I'll let myself into the room, and lie down beside you. I'll be there when you wake up...

And we'll be together, and I won't have been wrong—will I? It's still a miracle of sorts...regardless of the outcome. I am in this quiet room where Paul spent his last night on this earth. I hear the owl outside the window, and the monks chanting across the courtyard.

There is together and together. Some souls can never be apart, notwithstanding time and distance and even death. I've always been with you, and so has Paul. Sam, I know this: I'll never leave you. I never could. It's Christmas Eve. And I'm on my way to you.

All my love,
Hadley

About the Authors

*

Luanne Rice is the author, most recently, of *Last Kiss* and *Light of the Moon*, among many *New York Times* bestsellers. She lives in New York City and on the Connecticut shore.

Joseph Monninger has published nine novels and three nonfiction books, including the memoir *Home Waters*, and has been awarded two National Endowment for the Arts fellowships. He lives and teaches in New Hampshire, where his family runs a sled-dog team.